# COULD BE TOUCHED

### A NOVEL

# JOHN BOWENS

*This novel is a work of fiction. Any references to real people, events, establishments, or locales are intended only to give the fiction a sense of reality and authenticity. Other names, characters, and incidents occurring in the work are either the product of the author's imagination or are used fictitiously, as those fictionalized events and incidents that involve real persons. Any character that happens to share the name of a person who is an acquaintance of the author, past or present, is purely coincidental and is in no way intended to be an actual account involving that person.*

**ISBN:** (13) 978-0-9853303-1-6
Cover design: www.mariondesigns.com
Inside layout: www.mariondesigns.com
Editor: Clyde Edey

Anybody Could Be Touched/John Bowens


Step Ya Game Up Publishing
P.O. Box 25578
Charlotte, NC 28229
www.stepyagameuppublishing.com

First Printing January 2016
Printed in U.S.A.
10   9   8   7   6   5   4   3   2   1

# This Book is Dedicated To:

My sister, Edith "Crystal" Howard

STEP YA GAME UP PUBLISHING
EVEN FICTION NEEDS TO BE BELIEVABLE!

*...It doesn't matter who you are, at the end of the day...*

# Anybody
## COULD BE TOUCHED

A NOVEL

JOHN BOWENS

# Chapter One

It was easy to see how he got the name Mega Bucks! Ramel rushed out of Saks 5th Avenue with one light bag in his hand and an extra $4,200 due at the end of the month on his platinum American Express card.

It was already 2 PM and Ramel still had a dozen of things to do before his 6:15 flight to Miami departed.

Just as he attempted to flag down a cab, his phone began playing **Brooklyn's Finest** by Notorious B.I.G. featuring Jay-Z. Ramel snatched the phone from his hip and put it to his ear.

"Hello!"

"Yo' Ramel, what's up, it's Mike!"

"No shit, bird brain! I know who you are -- what's good?"

Ramel waved at a yellow cab, and it slowed down, but the driver took one look at Ramel's thug-ish appearance and put a heavy foot to the gas pedal.

"You faggot ass ma-fucker!!!" Ramel yelled.

"Damn son, why I gotta be all that?" Mike asked, sounding like a sad puppy.

"Man, I'm not even talking to you! A nigga tryna catch a cab."

"Oh ... You still bouncing to Miami tonight?"

"I don't know, I'm trying to… if I make it to the airport on time."

"Well if you don't for whatever reason, hit me up and let me know. I got a new artist I want you to hear."

"Alright son, I'll holla at you in a couple of hours." Ramel hung up before Mike got a chance to respond.

He began walking to the corner so he could catch a cab at the light and dee-bo his way into the back seat.

Just as Ramel made it to the corner, a candy apple red Bentley GT pulled up to the light sitting on 22 inch shiny chrome rims. Instinctively, Ramel made eye contact with the bad ass bitch that was driving. He smirked before acknowledging homie in the passenger seat gritting on him.

Before Ramel could avert his gaze and continue his search for a cab, homie in the passenger seat hollered his name.

"MegaBucks!"

Dude was smiling now!

Ramel ran through his mental rolodex, but couldn't place the face. Homie reached into the back seat of the GT and tossed a roll of Scott Toilet Tissue out the window. Not knowing what it was, Ramel caught it.

*What the fuck?!?* He thought as he realized what it was.

"Hold that for me, Baby-Boy!"

The light turned green, and the GT peeled off... but not before Ramel was able to catch the license plate number of the Bentley. Ramel was steaming!

He snatched his phone from his hip and quickly dialed a number.

"Hello, Deidra? Do me a favor ... have your sister run this license plate number for me."

Gina had a big ass mouth! Shorty couldn't keep a secret if her life depended on it. She was an expert at reciprocating information, and fortunately for her, there was always an ample amount of information to be reciprocated.

Gina was running around her apartment like a chicken with its head cut off. She was looking for her phone book. Today

she had hit the information jackpot, and she couldn't wait to spread the news!

This girl was so bad that she was probably the one who coined D.J. Clue's favorite saying on his mix tape; '*You know where you heard it first.*'

Gina found her phone book jammed between the cushions of her couch and she damn near tripped trying to get to the phone. She found Pauline's number and punched it in. The phone rang for an eternity! She hung up, and tried again. Still no answer.

"Damn!!!"

The sidewalk on Jamaica Avenue was congested as pedestrians made their way to and from their destinations. People was clothes shopping, Muslims was selling scented oils and incense, and high school kids was making their way to and from the bus terminal.

Big Time and his boys was at the entrance of the 165th street mall (the brick road) harassing people and trying to get as many female's phone numbers as possible. Gorgeous women were everywhere! Light skin, dark skin, slim, thick, and of various descents-- the mommies loved "the avenue."

"Shorty let me holla atchu a minute!" Big Time said, posting up like he was the smoothest nigga in the world.

Two cuties stopped in their tracks, uncertain of which one he was referring to. One was about 5'3" with a cinnamon complexion, a pretty face and a small waist, but the ass was like whoa! The other one was about the same height, but she was darker than night. Big Time thought her little black ass was sexy like a ma-fucker!

"No disrespect boo, but I like my women like my momma like her coffee, black and sweet! What's your name, sexy?"

Big Time scored big with shorty! So many men opted for light skin women that she was almost certain that what they really wanted was a white girl.

"My name is Yvette," she said, smiling, revealing beautiful white teeth.

"You got a man," Big Time inquired getting straight to the point.

"No ... but does that matter?"

It was Big Time's turn to smile, revealing a mouth full of gold teeth. "Probably not, the way I'm feeling your sexy little ass," he admitted and then continued. "Why don't you give me your number so I can holla atchu later, and we can kick it then?"

"Give me a pen."

"Nah, just tell me the number so I can put it in my phone," Big Time said quickly pulling out his phone.

"That phone is probably full of girl's numbers," Yvette said as she told him her number. "And who am I expecting a phone call from?"

"Oh, you can expect a call from Big Time. Everybody calls me Big Time."

"Yeah I heard of you!" Yvette proclaimed.

"And that's not a bad thing, Boo. When it comes to South Side, Jamaica Queens, the people want me to be mayor."

"Okay Mr. Big Time, call me any time after nine."

"No doubt!"

No sooner than Yvette was out of sight, Big Time was shooting his game at another dame. He and his boys were good and drunk from drinking 40 ounces' of Olde English all day. Hanging on Jamaica Avenue was a favorite past time and something they looked forward to, because you never knew what was going to happen.

And this was the case when the candy apple red Bentley GT pulled up. A roll of Scott Toilet Tissue came zooming from the passenger side window and banged Big Time in the head.

When he turned around to see what the hell had happened, all he saw was the ass of the GT, and he could've swore he heard a mother fucker yell: "Bow down!!!"

Thinking fast, Gina called another one of her girlfriends. Someone answered on the second ring.

"Hello?"

"Lazette, it's me Gina!"

"Hey girl, what's up?"

"I'm trying to get in touch with Pauline, have you heard from her?"

"No ... why? What's up?"

"Nothing, I just need to get in touch with her. Do you have her mother's number?"

"Yeah, but I'm not giving it to you until you tell me what the hell is going on. I know you girl, and something is up."

"Lazette, you're a trip! If something was up you would be the first person I told. Now stop playing and give me her number."

Lazette wasn't totally convinced, but she gave Gina the number anyway. Gina ended their conversation abruptly and placed a call to Ms. Grant. To her dismay, Pauline had been there, but she had just left not more than twenty minutes ago.

Gina felt defeated, and she knew it was useless but she decided to try Pauline's home number one more time before she gave up.

Just the night before, cats was on the block shooting! Niggaz was getting low, Tonya from the fifth floor was looking out her window being nosy, and Ms. Nadine was on the phone calling the po-leece.

It was probably a petty dispute; but at the end of the day,

someone's child was deprived of life.

That was yesterday. Today everything was all love. The sun was shining, displaying its beauty. Little homies crowded the basketball courts striving to be the next Jordan. Blind and Patches were on Howard Avenue and Pacific street slap boxing. Audrey and her little friends was jumping double-dutch, and Don Chi-Chi was posted up next to a 1989 Acura Legend, bobbing his head to the sounds of a Willie Black mix tape.

The Acura Legend was white with a grey bottom, and it belonged to Cue, who was sitting on two milk crates getting his hair braided by his home-girl Mookie.

The homie Slugz was laying in the cut watching Shelly and Sheena dancing around, shaking their asses as if they were in a rap video.

This was the atmosphere in Brownsville. Don Chi-Chi took the blunt from behind his ear and fired it up. He took in his surroundings and he knew that shit had to change. He felt he had put in too much work to still be fucked up in the game. Everybody and their mothers had a seven series BMW or a phat ass SUV. And here he was, most of the time riding shotgun in his cousin Cues' Legend.

He took a long drag of the blunt and walked over and passed it to Cue.

"Puff, puff, pass nigga!"

"Ah, ahh, ahhh- puff, puff, pass nigga!" Cue agreed.

Cue was a good dude. He was a retailer. He bought cocaine wholesale and he sold it retail. He recently jumped from 250 to 500 grams, and he was pretty much content with working with a half of a key. '*Slow money is better than no money*' was Cues' motto.

As long as Cue was touching that cheddar, Don Chi-Chi was straight. Don Chi-Chi was privy to the combination of the safe, and he spent his cousin's money like it was his own. Cue and Don Chi-Chi shared everything except the same motto!

While Cue's motto was '*Slow money is better than no money,*' Don Chi-Chi's motto was '*God bless the child who has his own!*'

His motto resonated in his mind when he spotted the candy apple red Bentley GT creeping up in front of 2020 Pacific Street. A bad ass bitch was driving, but main man in the passenger seat is what caught Don Chi-Chi's attention. It only took a few seconds for it to register.

"Big homie!?!" Don Chi-Chi yelled, hoping his eyes weren't deceiving him. Main man in the passenger seat offered a sinister smile before responding.

"031 fool!"

"We don't say that no more, yo! But what's popping," Don Chi-Chi said as he approached the vehicle.

"Y'all don't say 031 no more???"

"Naw, big homie; I gotta hit you with the remix!"

"Oh yeah???" big homie said, studying Don Chi-Chi's appearance. "I see you out here shining. What you doing, hustling?"

"Nah big homie, don't judge a book by its cover, the kid is fucked up! I mean, my cousin be out here grinding a little something, but other than that, shit is out of order."

"Oh yeah???"

"Word to blood! I was just thinking about how fucked up shit is before you pulled up. A nigga gotta get right."

"What you doing later on?"

"I'm doing whatever you tryna do!"

"Alright, bet! Meet me right here at ten o' clock tonight, ya heard?"

"No doubt, big homie. It's good to see you!" Don Chi-Chi said raising up from the window.

All eyes were on the GT! Mookie stopped doing Cue's hair, Shelly and Sheena stopped dancing, Audrey and her little friends dropped the jump rope and ran over to see for themselves the car that was straight out of a rap video, and Blind and Patches stopped slap boxing.

For the moment, Don Chi-Chi felt like the ultimate ghetto-star... until Big homie tossed him a roll of Scott Toilet Tissue and told him to "hold that!"

Gina jumped up and down like a fourth grader and squealed with delight when Pauline answered the phone.

"Pauline, I'm so glad I caught you. I was calling everybody trying to find you!"

"Who is this?" Pauline asked, not bothering to hide her annoyance.

"Oh, this is Gina... Lucky's friend."

"I'm burnt out girl, I didn't even recognize your voice. Now what got you all excited, you sound like you're about to pee in your pants?"

"Pauline, you're not going to believe who just came home!"

"Home? From where, the army?"

"Nooooooo! From lock down!"

"Oh, I told you I'm burnt out... Who?"

"Guess???"

"Who the hell is Guess?"

"No, I want you to guess who just came home."

"Girl, I ain't into no guessing games, who is it, Don John?"

"Nope!"

"Ivan???"

"Nope."

"Well, tell me already!"

"No, I want you to guess. You know this person real good."

Don Chi-Chi held the toilet tissue in his hand, and on his face was a look of total confusion.

8

"Fuck is this for, big homie?"

Big homie was waiting to hear that question all day, and he had the punch line ready. "Hold that for me, fool! I'm shitting! I'm gonna need that when I get back so I can wipe my ass!"

"Gina, I don't have time for this right now. Who is it, 'Preme?"

"Noooooo!"

"Well tell me because I have things to do."

"It's your brother's friend!"

"My brother has a thousand friends!!!"

Don Chi-Chi had to laugh! This nigga was in a Bentley GT about to change the whole game, and he was passing out toilet tissue.

"Ah, ahh, ahhh!!! I'm feeling you big homie! Get ya shine on! Blood rule, ya heard!?!"

Big homie was nonchalant. "Nah fool… Jerry Moore rule!"

"Who is it Gina???" Pauline was beginning to get upset.

"You know who it is!" Gina yelled, also getting upset because Pauline was too burnt out to guess the right answer.

"Obviously I don't. And if you're not going to tell me, then I'm about to hang up," Pauline threatened.

"O'kay, o'kay! You ready?"

"Gina!"

"It's Jerry Moore! Jerry Moore just came home on appeal!"

# Chapter Two

Chandar pushed the black SL 600 through the streets of downtown Los Angeles with a sense of urgency. He had the top down, and Tony Toni Tone could be heard with clarity blaring from the upgraded sound system.

*"It never rains in Southern California, they tell me-- it never rains in Southern California."*

It was after 4 PM and Chandar was late for an appointment with Jeff White, the new C.E.O. of Colossal Publishing. Chandar had developed a rapport with Jeff White two years ago when Mr. White was just an editor with a huge gambling habit.

While Chandar was still managing Club International on the outskirts of Las Vegas, Mr. White was known to frequent the establishment and lose an average of ten to fifteen grand per visit. Chandar couldn't understand how he managed to do this on an editor's salary.

One day while Mr. White was down on his luck, Chandar sent him a bottle of their best champagne, courtesy of Club International. He also sent Shakira, one of the girls that worked for him, over to keep Mr. White company. Shakira was Cuban American with an exotic look that could make the biggest loser feel as if he was winning.

Mr. White may not have been a rocket scientist, but it didn't take a wizard to figure out that Chandar was the one to thank for the champagne and the female companionship. At the end of the night, he took the time to express his gratitude.

"Mr. Grant?"

Chandar was at one of the cashier cages analyzing a ledger. He looked up when he heard his name being called.

"High roller! What can I do for you," Chandar asked with a pleasant demeanor.

"I just wanted to thank you for the champagne," Mr. White responded with a courteous smile, and then continued. "And Shakira showed me a wonderful time. I wanted you to know that I'm truly grateful."

Mr. White extended his hand, and Chandar gave it a firm shake.

"Just doing my job, Mr…"

"Oh! White… Jeff White! I must've loss my manners in that last big pot."

"That ain't about nothing Playboy. The way you be spending chips, I'm positive that whatever you lost is peanuts compared to what's left in the stash."

"Shiiiiiiit! At the rate I'm going, I'll be lucky if I have a place to stay at the end of the month."

"It couldn't possibly be that bad."

"Yeah it is. But I'm from the ol' dirty, so I'm use to climbing from the bottom," Mr. White said, automatically reverting to a southern drawl.

"Where at in the dirty?" Chandar asked, truly interested despite the pile of paperwork that needed his attention.

"Oh, I'm from the ol' ATL!"

"Atlanta? Where at in Atlanta???"

"College Park!"

"Get the fuck out of here. My dawg lives in CP!" Chandar exclaimed, then continued. "You ever heard of a place called Eddies'

"Are you serious? Eddies' is the only name brand in gold teeth! I got this gold tooth right here from Eddies'," Mr. White said, opening his mouth and pulling on his bottom lip.

"Small world!" Chandar said, and then continued. "Me

and Eddie go back like car seats in Land Cruisers."

"But wait a minute, I thought Eddie was from New York?"

"He is!"

"So…"

"Player, you don't hear my accent?"

"Dammit man, you from New York!"

And that was how Chandar and Jeff White became associates. On later visits, Chandar would learn that Jeff was an editor with Colossal Publishing. It just so happened that one of Chandar's homies, Makavelli, had written a book. The only thing was, Jeff edited books from the genre of Mysteries and Horror, while Makavelli's work was considered Urban fiction. Jeff didn't think that Urban fiction was a lucrative market.

"You gotta be kidding me," Chandar said one night after approving a $40,000 credit advance for Mr. White. "You're not familiar with *The Coldest Winter Ever* by Sister Soulja, or that joint by Teri Woods, *True to the Game*? That's a whole new monster; they call it Hip Hop fiction."

Jeff was still irresolute, but he told Chandar that he would review Makavelli's book.

The following week after reviewing the book, Jeff White introduced the idea of Hip Hop fiction at the weekly editors meeting. Two nights before, he had e-mailed copies of Makavelli's manuscript, titled 'Only God Can Judge Me,' to a couple of editors that he was cool with, for review. Although the idea for publishing Hip Hop fiction was met with disdain, one of the editors that had a chance to review *Only God Can Judge Me* thought the manuscript was highly marketable. The other editor that Jeff had e-mailed a copy, also admitted the book was pretty good. Ultimately, the senior editor, Bobbie Howard, gave the green light to publish *Only God Can Judge Me*, and the book went on to become an Essence #1 best seller.

This was the move that catapulted Jeff White to senior

editor status of his own department. Urban/ Hip Hop fiction had made its mark at Colossal Publishing, and Jeff went on to publish such authors as Toylin Henry, Corey Ford, A. Tyson, and a host of other bestselling authors. That was Jeff White's beginning in his rise to becoming C.E.O. of Colossal Publishing.

When Chandar pulled into a parking space in front of the building that held the offices of Colossal Publishing, his thoughts were interrupted by the soft ringing of the car phone. He looked at the caller I.D. and saw that the call was coming from New York.

"A-Blood, what's poppin' fool?" Chandar asked, wondering what the nature of the phone call was. A-Blood would normally only call if something big happened, or if he had something he wanted to get rid of, like guns, drugs, or counterfeit money. Back in the day, when Chandar was the head of the New York Bloods, he may have been interested, but nowadays he didn't want anything to do with it.

"Ah, ahh, ahhh!!! Ghetto Superstar, it be Blood poppin' and foes droppin', ya heard?!?"

"I heard!!!" Chandar said looking at his watch.

"Moreless, what's good in the sunshine state?"

"Ain't shit, nigga. I'm 031 minutes late for an important meeting," Chandar responded dropping back into the lingo, but still giving A-Blood a time check.

"My bad homie, go do what you gotta do and I'll get back with you later. Ya heard?"

"Nah, I can talk. Fuck is up wit' you?"

"I'm just trying to stay sucker free for-real, for-real. I was checking on you to see if anything new was going on."

Now Chandar was suspicious! '*This nigga A-Blood is fishing!*' "Anything new like what," Chandar asked, sounding nonchalant.

"Just anything," A-Blood said, and then continued. "Go 'head and take care of your biz, and holla at a nigga when you get a chance… ya heard?"

"I heard!" Chandar said, kinda annoyed from the little game they just played.

He hung up the phone and continued on his way to meet with Jeff White. It wasn't until after the meeting, while he was on his way home, that A-Blood's phone call began to make sense. Chandar received an emergency call from his sister Pauline. Unlike A-Blood, Pauline got straight to the point.

"Guess what big brother—**JERRY MOORE IS HOME!!!**"

# *Chapter Three*

## 'The life of this world vanishes rapidly and changes suddenly...'

Those are the words that would resonate in Jerry Moore's head for days to come. The Imam (spiritual leader of the Muslims) in the United States penitentiary Canaan, Yahya Ruhani, was one of the few people that Jerry Moore actually respected, and one of Yahya's favorite sayings of the prophet Muhammad (peace and blessings be upon him) was: *'The life of this world vanishes rapidly and changes suddenly. Therefore, beware of its sweetness so as to avoid the bitterness of its depriving, and beware of its delights so as to avoid the pains that they lead to.'*

If Jerry Moore couldn't identify then, he sure nuff could identify now! It all became clear to him... *'The life of this world vanishes rapidly...'*

Yesterday was gone, never to be seen again, and a lot of time had been wasted.

*'...and changes suddenly.'*

In one instant he was a prisoner with a plethora of restrictions, today he was a free man.

Jerry Moore was in Denise's basement apartment going over his plans. Denise was his ride or die chick! She didn't snitch like that bitch ass nigga Born! She stood up and faced the music, and the judge sentenced her to 36 months. She was released from Danbury Federal Correctional Institution over a year ago after serving 85% of her time.

Jerry Moore had asked his road dawg, Chandar, to look out for Denise, but obviously this request was denied. Denise was forced to live in the basement of her parents' home, and she was lucky to get a job at Home Depot.

This wasn't the only grievance Jerry Moore had with Chandar. Jerry Moore was livid that most of the homies in the 'hood was doing bad. Sure nuff gangstaz that put in work for the team was living fucked up, while Chandar and a chosen few were on the west coast getting chubby, doing the damn thing!

Jerry Moore snapped out of his reverie as Denise came out of the bathroom with a towel wrapped around her curvaceous body. She noticed Jerry Moore sitting on the pull-out couch with a troubled expression on his face.

"What's wrong, boo," she asked with a troubled expression of her own.

"Ain't shit, I was just thinking."

"About what?" Denise sat on the couch bed next to him, and just that quick, the big homie's thoughts switched gears! True, he was upset about some of the things he learned since he touched down, but damn, he was easily more concerned with the peach fragrance emanating from Denise's body. At least for now.

"All that's irrelevant," Jerry Moore said, gliding his hand over her thighs and under her towel. At the same time, he leaned over and threw some tongue in her mouth. Denise couldn't argue with that! She spread her legs apart and gave her lover access granted to the cookies. Jerry Moore couldn't believe that he was actually home, about to get his nuts out the sand.

He let his fingers explore Denise's hot, wet pussy until he found the button. He knew he was at the right address because Denise was all up in his ear telling him that he was.

"Oooooooooh Jerry, right there Daddy!" She was grinding against his fingers, and he was rotating in sync. Jerry Moore felt his dick urgently pressing against his pants, but he let it be all about Denise for the time being. He let his thumb put pressure and play with the clit while sliding two fingers inside her. Denise threw her head back and passionately fucked his fingers. She grinded and swooped until she came to a shaking climax! Jerry Moore looked down at her and smiled with a knowing look.

"Damn Daddy," she said, sounding exerted.

Jerry Moore stood up and slowly began to undress. Denise was watching him with pent up desire in her eyes. When Jerry Moore removed his shirt, it was as if his chest and stomach was chiseled. It was clear that the big homie had punished his body with a strict exercise program. Next, his pants came down, and Denise was overly attentive as the Mandingo saluted her and stood at attention. In fact, Denise climbed further on the bed, losing her towel, and began fingering herself and playing with her clit. Jerry Moore stepped out of his trousers and just stood there watching her. Their eyes locked while he stroked the one eye monster slowly. No words needed to be spoken! Denise quickly turned on her stomach, ass in the air, spreading her ass cheeks invitingly. She put her arm under her and between her legs stroking a finger across the crack of her ass and plunging it inside her soaking wet pussy. Jerry Moore had seen enough! He got on the bed with his knees and made his way over to Denise. He took his rock hard, pre-cum dripping dick, and slapped her ass with it.

"Stop playing, Jerry... fuck this pussy," she said, daring him.

He let the head glide in first, probing. Denise sucked in air hungrily.

"Stop... playing, please... pa-leeeeze."

He pushed further inside.

"Daddy... I miss yoooou... fuck this pussy!"

He pushed further and Denise lifted up and swooped the dick all the way in.

"Ahhhh.... yes Jerry... thank you," she cried. Jerry Moore began slapping rock-hard, backed-up dick like it was going out of style. He was massaging ass cheeks, playing with the asshole, and Denise was taking the dick like a champ!

Jerry Moore chased her off the bed with power strokes, but he wouldn't let her get away. He kept pounding the pussy as she crawled around on the floor as if she were trying to escape. And she had that look on her face! That 'I gotta take a shit' look'!

Denise couldn't remember the last time she came so hard! And when it was over, her pussy was throbbing!

Jerry Moore, sweating and exhausted, made his way to the tiny bathroom and jumped in the lukewarm shower. *'Damn! The water don't even get hot in this ma-fucker,'* he thought as he quickly washed up. *'Chander got my bitch living fucked up like we're in the seventies or some shit! It's all good though-- it's about to be some major changes!'*

Jerry Moore got out the shower, dried off, and then made his way back into the room, but Denise was now nowhere to be found. Instead, A-Blood stood in the middle of the room talking on his cell phone, clutching a green and black knapsack. When Jerry Moore entered the room, A-Blood ended his call.

"Ah, ahh, ahhh! Ghetto love, ghetto star!" A-Blood yelled.

"No doubt, Dawg! I know you didn't come for the car. I got that for the week!"

"Nigga, fuck that car! I came to kick it with my ma-fucking man!" A-Blood said, tossing the knapsack to Jerry Moore.

"What's this? And where Denise go?" Jerry Moore asked, putting the knapsack down and slipping some clothes on.

"She went upstairs to her mom's crib."

Jerry Moore put on a valuer, white and red John Tarik

sweat suit and some crisp white on white Air Force Ones. Not being able to take the suspense any longer, he snatched the knapsack and opened it up. A-Blood was watching him, smiling.

"Dammit man! The root of all evil." Jerry Moore said, sticking his face in the bag inhaling deeply. "How much is it?"

"That's forty grand right there. I figured that should hold you for now."

"Yeah, that's love… *for now*," Jerry Moore said, walking over and embracing A-Blood. "Real niggaz do real things, ya heard?"

"I heard, nigga! That's my word. I still can't believe you're home!"

"I was just thinking the same thing."

"Come on, let's go take a ride. I got something else for you too!"

A-Blood took Jerry Moore to a garage in the Bronx. He made him close his eyes as he used a remote control to open the garage door.

"Matter of fact, turn around- don't open your eyes!" He had his hands on Jerry Moore's shoulders, " O'kay, now walk backward … keep going … keep going … bang! Open your eyes!!!"

A-Blood was holding two motorcycle helmets. Jerry Moore turned around and was face to face with a fleet of dirt bikes, motorcycles, and four wheelers. All of the bikes looked inviting, but the two that stood out was Chandar's red Suzuki GSX R1300 Hayabusa, and the red and black R1 that Jerry was only privileged to see in pictures that he received while in prison.

"Dammit man," he said as he grabbed one of the helmets from A-Blood.

Each bike already had the keys in the ignitions, so all Jerry Moore had to do was choose his weapon and crank it up!

He chose the Hayabusa, so A-Blood manned up the R1 and they set out to enjoy an old ritual.

In the Bronx, they tore ass down Jessup Avenue, provoked the police on Boston Road, made their way to 161st Street and zipped pass Yankee Stadium on their way to the Third Avenue Bridge.

The Polo Grounds went by like a blur, but they slowed down on 125th Street in Harlem. Jerry Moore couldn't believe how much things had changed. The only thing that didn't change was the fact that the city was alive! New York was still the city that didn't sleep!

For the spectators, Jerry Moore and A-Blood threw the bikes up and wheelied for blocks down 145th Street. They stopped on 8th Ave and acted a fool for the small crowd in front of Willie Burgers.

Then they were hitting the Triboro Bridge which took them to the Brooklyn Queens Expressway, and they were making their presence felt in Bedstuy, Fort Green, Flatbush, and grimy ass Brownsville.

On Linden Blvd they breezed through East New York and stopped at a gas station to fill their tanks before bouncing to Queens.

Jerry Moore felt like he died and went to heaven! His adrenaline was flowing and it felt good to be home.

They rode through 40 projects, Baisley and Rochdale. Jerry Moore wanted to hit Woodside, Astoria, and Queens Bridge, but A-Blood had taken the lead and led them to Far-Rockaway. They whizzed pass Red Fern and Edgemere, and went up the ramp leading to the boardwalk. A-Blood did an indo balancing himself on the front wheel with the rear wheel in the air, and Jerry Moore began doing donuts holding the front brake while revving the gas and letting the back wheel spin in circles. The sand from the beach was flying everywhere.

A-Blood and Jerry Moore parked their bikes on the

boardwalk and climbed up on a lifeguard post to take a break. The wooden platform seat was big enough for two people.

The sound of the waves crashing against the shore was peaceful, and although both gangstaz would've preferred the company of some bad bitches, both were content to be in each other's presence. This was homie time!

"Dammit man, this is beautiful! I feel good like a ma-fucker!" Jerry Moore yelled as they stared into the darkness of the Atlantic Ocean.

A-Blood took a snub nose 357 magnum from an ankle holster and placed it in his lap. He looked around, surveying their surroundings for any potential danger.

"It's your time to shine, big dawg! But the question is, what you tryin' to get into?"

Jerry Moore was silent. For the past three and a half years, all he did was exercise and study the law. His plan was to stay healthy and find a way to make it back to society. The 360 months that the judge sentenced him to serve in federal prison was so imposing that it was difficult to see past it. Anyone who has been to trial defending their self against the federal government knows that the fight is tantamount to that of David and Goliath.

Seeing that an immediate answer wasn't forthcoming, A-Blood decided to offer some assistance.

"The way I see it is like this. Your transition shouldn't be difficult. I got your back, and you know Chandar got her back. You just have to acclimate.

With that, Jerry Moore was overcome by ambivalence. It felt good as shit to be home, but at the same time, he was becoming depressed because he didn't know what the fuck to do next.

"I know y'all got my back, dawg. But still, it's not like I have a long list of options."

"Sure you do! Chandar got the club in Vegas, plus he

got his foot in the door at Colossal Publishing. I'm fucking with Real estate and stocks. I could teach you how to invest, or I could hook you up with my people at Loud Mouth Records."

"All that shit sound good A; BUT, and this is no disrespect, I'm not trying to be in Chandar's shadow, and I'm damn sure not trying to impose on you. I need my own hustle!"

"And all that will come in time, it's no rush! You got 40 grand already, and you know…"

"That's what I'm talking about!" Jerry Moore said cutting A-Blood off, " I'm not trying to have my hand out like a bitch, I'm a man first! And on some real shit, that 40 grand ain't enough for a 10% down payment on the car I want… Let's not talk about my living arrangements."

A-Blood was hardly one to be at a loss for words, but Jerry Moore's last statement sent him into a zone of silence.

"I'm a big boy, A! And big boys don't wait for shit to happen, they make shit happen!"

There was a brief moment of silence and A-Blood shook his head, "So I'm gonna ask you again… What you trying to get into?"

"You know what I'm trying to get into," Jerry Moore said raising his voice. "Street life, nigga!" then he dropped his voice into a whisper. "It's the only life I know."

A-Blood watched his homie with concern. The idea that prisons were built to rehabilitate criminals was nothing but a farce! A-Blood knew from experience that prisons lacked educational programs, vocational programs were obsolete, and the only criminals likely to change for the better was the small percentage who knew that change was necessary. Other than that, on a large scale, prisons did nothing but promote recidivism!

"Homie… I feel your pain but… I can't support that decision. Chandar won't support-"

"Fuck Chandar! Everybody always saying Chandar this, Chandar that! He's not my mutha fuckin' father! I love the homie, and I got love for you, A! But if niggaz ain't with me then they against me! Straight like that!"

"I'm just saying –"

"The streets need me, A! Homies is fucked up! Gansta ass niggas are doing bad!"

"I'm just saying, homie."

"You're just saying what? You said you got my back…"

"And I do!"

"Then hold me down no matter what decision I make. Dammit man."

A-Blood just stared out into the darkness in defeat. Jerry Moore was home, and it was just matter of time before the gritty streets of New York was transformed into a battlefield.

# Chapter Four

His hood' was a haven for dudes who liked to shut down whole strips! They pushed the hottest whips, sexed the hottest chicks, wore the hottest jewels, and put pressure on the other 'hoods.

These dudes pushed nickels of crack, buy one get one free for a month straight to gain clientele. They stuck hot curling irons up people's butts to set examples. These guys killed people, chopped up dead bodies, popped champagne, then slept like babies.

These are the elements that molded Blueberry-Loc! These were the people that he wanted to emulate; thus, he became a product of his environment.

Blueberry-Loc looked out the window for the hundredth time when he finally spotted the super stretch limousine creeping to the curb in front of 97-15 Waltham Street. He made his way outside, nonchalantly, and walked to the Nissan Path Finder that pulled up directly behind the limo.

Blueberry-Loc had a unique walk. It was actually a combination of a limp and a hop, and it was the result of a severe ass kicking that left him with broken bones and a damaged spinal cord. He stayed in a coma for three weeks and doctors predicted that he would never walk again. They were wrong!

The owner of the limousine service jumped out of the

jeep smiling from ear to ear, and he embraced Blueberry-Loc as if they were old friends.

"I personally made sure your ride was on time," he said, glancing at his watch.

"Good looking, Cuz! I plan on doing it real big tonight," Blueberry-Loc said as he reached in his pocket and pulled out a stack of cash. He peeled off a crisp one hundred dollar bill and passed it to the man.

The man took the bill and made it disappear in his pocket just as the chauffeur of the limo approached them.

"This here is Guy! He's going to be your driver for the night. Guy, allow me to introduce you to the birthday boy, Blueberry-Loc! He gets VIP treatment! Let me explain the protocol real quick... there's an intercom system in the back that gives you access to communicate with Guy at any time. When you want to stop somewhere, pick up the phone! You have a change of plans, pick up the phone! Any problem at all, all you have to do is pick up the phone! Whenever you reach an intended destination, Guy won't get out of the vehicle until you pick up the phone and give the order. After you give the order, Guy will come around and tap on your window three times. He won't open the door to let you out until you return the tap! Your bar is full. You have twelve bottles of Cristal, and twelve bottles of Alize' chilling on ice in the back... Guy has another supply up front in case you run low. All your controls: TV, DVD, lights, air condition, all that is easy to use. Guy... you want to add anything?"

Guy was a big person; he weighed in the neighborhood of three hundred and fifty pounds. He literally had to take a deep breath before speaking.

"Just a few things. I'm glad to offer my services Mr. Blueberry-Loc, and I want you to have a great birthday. I only ask that no one hangs out of the windows, or the sunroof. Besides that, the boss basically summed everything up."

Blueberry-Loc held out his hand to the owner and gave him a firm handshake.

"I appreciate you dropping by personally to make sure everything is alright. We can definitely do business again."

"That's what I like to hear!"

After wrapping up the formalities, Blueberry-Loc made his way back inside the house to dress properly for a night on the town. He put on a powder blue E.C. sweater from the Exclusively Crystal Collection, a pair of baggy E.C. blue jeans, and powder blue Timberland Chucks. He wore a baby blue and white Avirex leather jacket, and a platinum wrist watch designed by John Tarik; but the eye catcher was the medallion swinging on the platinum chain that his Uncle Ray copped for him for his birthday. The medallion was a stick up kids' fantasy! It was the shape of an octagon, displayed an emblem of a scale, signifying justice, and it was shrouded with a sequence of diamonds and sapphire. Uncle Ray spent about a hundred and fifty grand for the medallion alone. Blueberry-Loc sported a bracelet that matched the chain, and a pinky ring that was absolutely frozen!

He stepped out the crib feeling like the mutha-fucking president!

Big guy was standing at attention by the rear door of the limo until he saw Blueberry-Loc hobbling out the house. He quickly opened the door for the birthday boy. Blueberry- Loc floated into the backseat of the limo and looked around. While the exterior of the limo was eggshell white, the interior was sky blue plush leather, with dark blue heart shaped pillows.

Blueberry-Loc had to smile. He was satisfied. He automatically picked up the phone and barked instructions.

"115-53 227th Street!"

They had to pick up his man Strobe, who was designated to handle security for the night. Then he wanted to briefly stop by Karen's Soul Food Restaurant on Queen's Blvd.

Karen was a bad chick! She had the type of body that made a nigga's dick jump involuntarily. She was obviously independent, and she possessed a ride or die mentality. But these weren't the reasons that Blueberry-Loc was checking for shorty. Blueberry-Loc was on some straight up plotting shit, and he needed to cut into Karen bad! Karen was sleeping with the enemy! Blueberry-Loc got word that this bad bitch who owned a soul food restaurant on Queens Blvd, was in direct contact with the slobs that tried to kill him.

He played with the medallion resting against his solar plexus and thought about the jewel his Uncle Ray had dropped on him earlier that day.

"Boy, close your eyes!" Uncle Ray demanded. They were in the living room of the house that Ray owned in the Bay Chester area of the Bronx. Blueberry-Loc closed his eyes, and Ray pulled out the platinum chain and medallion, and placed it around his nephews' neck.

"O'kay, look it here."

Blueberry-Loc opened his eyes, and they widened like a child seeing a bird fly for the first time.

"Oh, shit!"

"Watch your mouth boy, I'm still your uncle! You see the scale? Well, that signifies justice. Do you know what karma is, Kevin? It means that whatever people do in their life, good or bad, it comes back to them. I'm glad that you're well, and I hope your therapy is successful, but always remember this ... justice will prevail! What goes around comes around! So I don't want you wasting valuable time and energy focusing on the people who hurt you. Please Kevin! It you need anything, don't hesitate to ask. Your family is here for you, o'kay? Happy birthday, nephew!"

As the limousine jetted through the streets of Queens, Blueberry-Loc could hear his uncle's voice echoing in his head. As he looked at the scale shrouded with diamonds and sapphire, his eyes became watery. He knew his uncle was right, but sometimes justice had to be pursued. Blueberry-Loc wasn't quite prepared to leave it in the hands of fate. Niggaz had left him for dead!

After they picked up Strobe, it only took about fifteen minutes before they were pulling up in front of Karen's Soul Food Restaurant. Blueberry-Loc and Strobe were shooting the breeze while they sat back watching *The Count of Monte Cristo* on DVD. Blueberry-Loc let about five minutes pass before picking up the phone. "Let's do this!"

Guy's big fat ass was on automatic! He got out the limo and quickly made his way to the back door, tapping three times before standing at attention, and waiting for the birthday boy to return the tap.

A small crowd was forming on the sidewalk as curious pedestrians tried to steal a glance inside the limo. Blueberry-Loc could see the customers inside of Karen's restaurant breaking their neck's to see what was going on. Even Karen came to the large plate glass window to be nosey. Blueberry-Loc waited until two bad bitches came out the restaurant and stood to the side whispering, their eyes never leaving the limo, before he returned the tap.

Guy opened the door and Strobe was the first one out studying the terrain, before waving Blueberry-Loc out into the lime light.

Blueberry-Loc stepped out onto the sidewalk as if he were the superstar celebrity that all the people expected to see. He made his way to the entrance of the restaurant, slowing down long enough to offer a smile to the two dimes standing to the side.

"Damn! We thought you was Michael Jackson or somebody," one of them said as if she was disappointed.

Blueberry-Loc's smile widened. He winked his eye at shorty who remained quiet, and kept it moving.

Inside the restaurant, all eyes were on him! Blueberry-Loc was nonchalant as he searched for, and found, who he was looking for. Karen was standing next to the cashier station looking edible! Their eyes locked, and Blueberry-Loc closed the distance between them. He tried to read shorty's mind, but she was just standing there with a smirk.

"Where's my birthday present," Blueberry-Loc shot, putting her on the defensive.

"Oh, today's your birthday? That's why you're frontin', pulling up in a limo and whatnot, huh?"

"I told you I was gonna come through. You forgot, or you didn't take me serious?"

"To be honest with you, I really didn't take you serious."

"That's crazy! I think you did take me serious, you just didn't want to splurge and get the kid a gift."

"You're right about that. She's tighter than ten toes in a sock!" The two dimes from outside had found their way into close proximity, and they were all up in the business!

"Happy birthday," sang the one whom had remained quiet when they were outside.

"Thanx boo!"

"Why don't y'all mind your business? And I am not tight Gina, so you need to stop it," Karen said, folding her arms.

"I'll take a rain check on the gift..." Blueberry-Loc said, and then continued. "You wanna go for a ride?"

Karen put a beautifully manicured finger to her temple as if she was actually thinking about it.

"Blueberry-Loc, you are a gang banger... Where would you take me, to do a drive-by?"

That drew a wave of laughter from the two dimes, but Blueberry-Loc wasn't dissuaded.

"If that's what you're into, with me, we can do whatever, but that's not what I had in mind."

"Well, what exactly did you have in mind," Karen asked mockingly.

"Boo, my mind is artistic. I was just seeing pictures of you and I getting to know each other a little bit. If that's too heavy for you..."

Karen took a deep breath and exhaled slowly. "Listen bee... You're a street person-"

"And???"

"And I'm an entrepreneur-"

"And???"

"Well... The two don't mix. To be honest with you, I can never knowingly date a gang banger. I mean, a man with a little thug in him can be very attractive, but a full blown gang banger is a bit much for me."

"I see you enjoy judging a book by its cover."

"No, I just call it how I see it."

"I don't think we're getting anywhere with this conversation, and time is money so I think I'd better be going. But listen to me... I think you're beautiful, you're smart, independent, witty, and then some. You have all the qualities to make a street nigga, or any other kind of nigga, change his ways. Right now I don't know if we're compatible or not, but what I do know is this; I don't want to die until I find out. Give me a phone number or something. Let me call you."

"Bridgette, give me a pen." The girl at the cash register handed her a pen and a piece of paper. Karen scribbled on the paper quickly and handed it to Blueberry-Loc.

"What the hell is this?"

"What?"

"555-6000.

"Oh, that's the number to the restaurant."

"Boo, I'm not trying to order no food, I'm trying to holla!"

"Boy, please... I live in this restaurant. I'm here all day, every day, even on Sunday."

"Sounds like you could use some excitement in your life."

"My job is exciting."

"You got a comeback for everything!"

"Just about."

"Well, can I get a hug?"

Karen came forward and Blueberry-Loc smothered her with a big hug. Her fragrance was intoxicating and Blueberry-Loc almost forgot that he was a man on a mission. He pulled himself away.

"Take care of yourself, alright," he said to Karen. And to the nosey bitches, pretending not to be nosey, "Y'all be good!"

"O'kay!"

"Happy birthday!"

"Bye!"

When Blueberry-Loc exited the restaurant he had one thing on his mind, and it wasn't pussy. Guy had the back door to the limo open, and Strobe was posted up outside watching the surroundings. Blueberry-Loc floated into the plush back seat whispering the words: **'Justice will prevail!'**

# Chapter Five

*"Guess whose back in the mother fucking house…"* (The crowd screaming), **"With a fat dick for your mother fucking mouth!"**

The DJ was spinning an old Snoop-Dogg song from the Doggy style days, and the gees in the crowd was singing along. It was a Friday night, and they were having a gangsta party. Jerry Moore had only been home for a week, but A-Blood was able to pull together a host of homies to welcome him home in style.

They were at Travagar Square, a popular club in Queens that had the capacity to hold over a thousand party goers with no threat of safety inspectors shutting the joint down.

The bouncers had already broken up three fights on the dance floor, and provided medical attention to a guy who had been knocked over the head with a champagne bottle, and it wasn't even close to midnight.

The crowd outside was just as crazy as the crowd inside, hanging on and pulling on the awning that read, 'Travagar Square', damn near pulling it down. The personnel had to beef up security at the entrance, because people were pushing and shoving, threatening to bulldozer their way right through the front door. The cops couldn't even contain the crowd; and as a result, there were about a hundred cops on the block behind the club while the menacing crowd occupied the front.

Jerry Moore was standing up with his arms folded in an authoritative manner, looking out of the huge window up in VIP that provided a view of the entire club. He watched as A-Blood made his way through the crowd, stopping occasionally to talk to a homie or one of the tantalizingly beautiful women, before making a bee line for the staircase that led to the VIP. The chain around his neck holding the VIP pass made it a simple task to breeze past security and into the comfort zone of the VIP lounge.

There were only roughly ten to fifteen people in VIP; some occupied the bar, which was on one side of the room, others sat at tables or booths on the other side. A huge plasma playing music videos was on mute in one corner, and smaller screens were strategically placed throughout the lounge. The west wall was all glass and provided the view that Jerry Moore was now enjoying.

"Yo, these niggaz is wildin'," A-Blood said, pulling up to the window next to Jerry Moore. He quickly pointed to a spot on the dance floor. "Look at Don-Chi-Chi. He fuckin' wit' that little bitch from Rochdale that work in Green Acres Mall... What's her name?"

"Where?" Jerry Moore asked, scrutinizing the crowd as if he was trying to track an enemy.

"Right there fool, you blind like a ma-fucker," A-Blood said, pointing into the crowd.

"Oh... dammit man! What's shorty name? Latricia, Latasha... some shit like that. Send somebody to get her!"

"Be easy, fool, it's early. Come on, I wanna introduce you to Biz."

A-Blood and Jerry Moore made their way downstairs, and through the crazy crowd, headed toward the stage where Biz Markie was playing music. Jerry Moore ran into an abundance of familiar faces as the Dons and Divas in attendance paid homage.

One familiar face belonged to Chuck, an old cocaine supplier with whom Jerry Moore use to do business.

"Welcome home, big dawg," Chuck yelled over the music. Simultaneously, he reached into his inside pocket, and produced a fat envelope which he passed to Jerry Moore. "That's just a little contribution from the home team! My phone number is in there too. Holla atcha boy," he continued.

Jerry Moore didn't crack a smile. He just nodded his head stolidly.

When they finally made it to the stage, Biz Markie was playing *I'm fucking You Tonight* by the Notorious B.I.G. featuring R. Kelly. After A-Blood made the introductions, Biz grabbed the microphone and shouted: **"Jerry Moore is in the house! Show some love to the big homie ... Welcome home!"**

The crowded was going bananas! That's when one of the stage directors came and informed A-Blood that Willie Black and the 4-1-0 hustlers were backstage and they were ready to perform. Willie Black was an artist currently signed to Loud Mouth Records! In New York, he was one of the hottest rappers burning up the mix tape outlet, but the A&R at Loud Mouth had yet to make him a priority.

Biz Markie shut the music down and the stage director's killed the lights. A-Blood and Jerry Moore slid to the side as Willie Black's voice penetrated the club.

"First of all, I wanna send a shout out to my mutha fuckin' self, Willie Black!"

The crowd was confused at first, but when they recognized the familiar voice from the mix tapes, they began to go into a frenzy!

Cub, one of the members in the group, was screaming, **"4-1-0 hustlers in the building!"**

Then all at once, the lights came on, the beat dropped, and Willie Black started spitting lyrics; a mic in one hand, a bottle of Moet in the other.

*"Cops tryna knock me, Feds tryna case me, niggaz tryna rob me, the streets is crazy! Give me a sweet 380, Nina or a Glock Forty, Blaze ya block, leave ya team in the top story… you know me, nigga born average, came up in the hood then I reached don status—Willie Black! The milli in fact- be my right hand man, when you see Willie Black! Be silly and act like you can't get ya brains blown out, the top off-your ceiling and hat! If you feeling the rap, you probably stood on the corner- dealing them packs/ If not, you probably hot- or be dealing with rats! Make a million from crack, is a thug nigga fantasy/ It's over a million gats, that'll have you sleeping on your canopy/ Do whatever to the door that the fucking judge hand to me/ If I end up in the morgue, niggaz coming for ya family. / I done dealt with the hardships, headaches, and calamities. / Keep it gutter mutha fucka, so a nigga can't slander me! <u>Jerry Moore! What up, big homie!"</u>*

Jerry Moore had his game face on, so he just nodded his head in acknowledgment… but Willie Black's next words almost made his heart skip a beat!

**"Oh my God! The ghetto star, Chandar is in the building!"**

Jerry Moore was sure that his ears had deceived him! But sure enough, he turned his head, and right there on the stage he was face to face with Don Chi-Chi, Wild Blood, and the one and only, his partner in crime… Chandar!

KA-BOOM! The present reality invaded Jerry Moore's

36

existence like buckshot's from a 12 gauge shotgun. He'd been putting off the inevitable meeting with Chandar for a week now; he didn't exactly know why, but what he did know was that he needed some time to think.

Chandar was his road dawg, there was no doubt about that. They had been partners since adolescent years. They were friends when they were broke. They were together when they first started seeing some real money. Shit, they even became Blood together!

Still, Jerry Moore experienced a sense of ambivalence. On one hand, he was excited and happy to reunite with his homie whom had held him down like a blood relative while he was on lockdown, but on the other hand, he felt some kind of way about how Chandar had treated the homies on the east coast in general, and he was definitely tight about the Denise situation in particular. Beneath the surface, Jerry Moore's real problem was Chandar's status. Chandar was that nigga for real! He was a thinker, so he was able to escape the trap that the feds had set up, and which Jerry Moore had fell victim to. He was smooth and he had style, and everybody acknowledged him as the big homie. The fact was, Jerry Moore and Chandar were supposed to be partners, but it never failed, wherever they went, everyone always gave Chandar all the props. Chandar was the head nigga in charge!

Even now, they was on the stage, and the spotlight was on Chandar. Willie Black and the 4-1-0 Hustlers had ended their performance, and niggaz in the crowd was shouting out for... Chandar. A plethora of women resembling models rushed the stage, and they were vying for the attention of... Chandar. The photographer was on the scene, and everyone wanted to get in the pictures with... Chandar. This was supposed to be a 'Welcome Home' party for Jerry Mutha-Fucking Moore!

Never the less, Jerry Moore had his game face on! He'd

share the spotlight for now, but a whole lot of shit was about to change. Riding shotgun was for scrubs, and Jerry Moore was ready to drive! Perhaps this was the reason he didn't want Chandar to know he was home yet, but the truth was, there's always enough shine for everybody... Unfortunately, Jerry Moore wasn't hip to this.

Through the chaos, it was impossible for Chandar and Jerry Moore to communicate effectively, so they retreated to the preferable atmosphere of VIP. The bubbly was in abundance and heavy weed smoke was in the air. Only the baddest chicks in the club were allowed into what was now transferred into a private party. The little dime piece that Jerry Moore had his eye on earlier, whose name was actually Lashawn, may have been one of the baddest bitches in the room.

A-Blood, Don Chi-Chi, Wild-Blood, Willie Black, and the rest of the 4-1-0 Hustlers were trying to instigate a wet t-shirt contest, and in the corner of the room, Jerry Moore and Chandar were at a booth; laying in the cut like dried blood. Chandar was sipping on bottled water, but Jerry Moore had a magnum of Dom and he was getting his drink on.

"Jerry Miz-zoore, what's really good," Chandar began, watching his homie closely and studying his body language.

Jerry Moore was checking out the festivities going on around them, avoiding heavy eye contact with Chandar.

"You hear me, fool? This shit feel like a dream! I still can't believe I'm home."

"Well, it's not a dream. Jerry Moore is on the tiz-zown! My question to you is, and I would be remiss if I didn't ask ... how long was you planning on keeping me in the dark?"

Jerry Moore readjusted himself in his seat; for some reason he couldn't get comfortable. He knew he owed Chandar an explanation, but for the life of him, he couldn't think of anything that would be acceptable, and this frustrated him.

"I was gonna holla, I just… I don't know, I needed some time to get my head right. Dammit man, I wanted to surprise you."

"Oh yeah?!?" Chandar said somewhat sarcastically, and then continued. "Well, I would be remiss if I didn't admit that you definitely surprised me!"

"Listen homie… I would be remiss if I didn't tell you that I don't appreciate the way you're coming at me! You got a nigga feeling like he on supervised release or some shit; like I gotta report to you!"

"Hold up, player. I'm missing something here! Something is going over my head. My mutha fucking homie just came home. Together, me and my homie went to war with the U.S. government!! We used all of our resources, time, and energy to free my homie from the white man's modern day slavery. We did this together! And now my homie is free and I'm the last one to find out about it? And when I do find out, it's not from you???"

"What you want, an apology dawg?"

"Nah, playboy. I wanna know what the fuck is on ya mind… that's what men do, they speak their mind, bottom line!"

"You wanna know what's on my mind, dawg? You really want to know what's on my mind???"

Jerry Moore was facing his homie now, eyes locked, leaning on the table.

Chandar was calm, cool, and collected. He didn't blink!

"I just traveled from coast to coast for no other reason… speak ya mind."

One of Jerry Moore's eyes was squinting and the other was wide open, he normally reserved that look for when he was plotting or when an enemy was close by.

"You hear me, fool? Homies in the hood are fucked up! How you sending me pictures from Mexico, Europe, Jamaica, and Puerto Rico, standing in front of drop top Porsches and Lamborghini's with bitches that look like they don't speak English, and homies in the hood is starving? From what I understand, Don Chi-Chi put in some major work for the team… Why is he riding around in cabs? Why he don't have a decent place to live and a bank account? I asked you to look out for Denise. Shorty rode out for me, she blew trail and did time. Why is she living in her mom's basement?"

"Is that what this is really about, playa?" Chandar asked. This nigga Jerry Moore was acting like a bitch! He was acting like he no longer respected Chandar's mental. Chandar was always the thinker, Jerry Moore was the strength! Now, Jerry Moore must've went to prison and found a brain. Unbelievable!

First of all, niggaz in the hood was fucked up because they chose to be. Chandar had reached out time and time again, he was still reaching out, but niggaz didn't want a helping hand, niggaz wanted to pimp!

Did Don Chi-Chi tell Jerry Moore about the Five Series BMW that Chandar gave him, and which he wrecked in less than a months' time… probably not. Did he even tell him about the fifteen grand that Chandar gave him whenever he was in New York (which wasn't much, but still…) probably not. And Denise? That bitch was ride or die alright… she offered to ride Chandar's dick like he never had it rode before! Chandar had tried to look out for shorty, but she misread him. She thought he was pushing up on her, and she was all for it.

Chandar didn't feel he had to explain these things to his homie, he felt that Jerry Moore knew him well enough to respect his gangsta.

"You know the rules, playboy; never let a bitch come between gangstaz!"

Jerry Moore, already upset, took that the wrong way and responded with venom before he could catch himself.

"That rule didn't apply when *your bitch* was alive."

Jerry Moore was referring to Chandar's baby's mother, Lisa. She was killed during a kidnapping that went bad. That was a long time ago, but Chandar was still in the healing process. He snatched Jerry Moore's magnum of Dom and smashed it against the wall! They both stood up staring at each other threateningly.

Don Chi-Chi was one of the first ones alerted that something was wrong… Eager to prove his loyalty to Jerry Moore, he reached for the 9mm on his waist, but A-Blood stopped him.

"Be easy, fool!"

"Man, I'm rolling with the big homie!" Don Chi-Chi yelled.

"They're both big homies!" A-Blood reminded him.

Wild Blood heard Don Chi-Chi's statement and was upset that he didn't bring his own burner. Don Chi-Chi had made a big mistake by choosing sides; one way or the other.

Chandar had fire in his eyes! He looked around and observed the audience all up in their business.

"It's not a good time for this…" he said, and then continued. "But we definitely have some unfinished business to take care of, believe that! Wild Blood, we out! A-Blood be easy!"

Chandar grabbed his water and took a sip before smashing the plastic bottle against the wall… Water sprayed a few people sitting nearby. Then he gangsta strolled out of VIP like he wished a mother fucker would object to his behavior.

Jerry Moore didn't like the way his conversation with Chandar had went, but he felt the homie had cracked slick first. He was in a sour mood so he proceeded to get drunk, and the more intoxicated he got, the more arrogant he became. A-Blood tried to advise him that it wasn't that big, and that him and Chandar needed to talk it out. A-Blood was neutral! On the other hand, Don Chi-Chi was openly pledging allegiance to Jerry Moore. That may not have been a wise thing to do, but Jerry Moore did nothing to discourage him. Instead, Jerry Moore was feeling himself at an all-time high. The music penetrated VIP, but it wasn't as loud as it was throughout the rest of the club. Never the less, it was loud enough for Lashawn and her girlfriends from section 5 in Rochdale. Now that most of the tension was gone, they began to dance among themselves, trying to enjoy the party. Lashawn knew that Jerry Moore was watching her even though she pretended she didn't. Throughout the night she had time to do a little homework on him, and she learned that Jerry Moore was a baller. Lashawn thought he was cute too; that was a plus. Now she was just waiting for him to make a move. It was ironic how guys would think that they were the ones that did the choosing, when in actually, majority of the times they were chosen. A man would never admit that a woman could pimp just as hard, if not harder, than the average man.

"Ayo, Don Chi-Chi... You hear me fool," Jerry Moore said, sunk down in the booth, mesmerized by the way Lashawn was moving her hips.

"What's popping, big homie?"

"You see shorty right there with the pink top?"

"Who Lashawn?"

"Yeah, that's her name."

"Shorty badder than all outdoors, and them Apple Bottom jeans look good as shit!"

"Yeah, yeah. Go tell shorty to come here."

Don Chi-Chi wasn't feeling that, but he didn't let it show. He did what he was told! On the low, he had planned on being the one leaving with shorty, now he had to change the plan.

Lashawn though it was tacky that Jerry Moore didn't approach her himself, but she went along with the program because if she waited for a nigga to do something right, it probably wouldn't happen. That was the reason Lashawn always kept a girl on the side, a woman would always know what a woman likes.

"Hi," She said in a melodic voice as she approached the booth.

"What up, ma! You tryin' to chill with me for the night?"

*'No this nigga didn't!'* Lashawn thought. *'Niggaz don't know what to say out their mouth.'* But she had already decided that she was going to chill with him for the night, so he was already chosen!

"Let me say bye to my girlfriends."

"Be ready when I get back. I got something I need to take care of myself." Jerry Moore said arrogantly.

Jerry Moore grabbed Don Chi-Chi and A-Blood, and they went downstairs to the dance floor. They made their way through the crowd, and the next thing you know, they was at the stage. A-Blood didn't know what the homie was up to, but he knew that he would soon find out.

Jerry Moore commandeered the stage and had Biz Mark stop the music. He grabbed the microphone, and like a true gangsta, he began to address the crowd.

**"Where Damu at?"** he yelled.

Damu is Swahili for blood! The crowd was buggin' off Jerry Moore stopping the music, but some of the Bloods was responding.

**"We right here, dawg!"**

Jerry Moore wasn't satisfied with that response!

**"Ayo! Hold the fuck up! I know it's more gangstaz in the building than that! Where the fuck is my dawgs at???"**

Now shit started getting crazy! Niggaz were barking, and a little pushing and shoving began as the Bloods tried to get closer to the stage to support the big homie. "Woof... woof... woof... woof... woof!"

Niggaz was banging on shit, and at this point, anybody who wasn't Blood had to be feeling uncomfortable. Lashawn was at the window up in VIP with her friends looking at Jerry Moore as if he lost his mind.

**"Dammit man! That's what the fuck I'm talking about! Y'all feeling this Blood shit?"**

The dawgs was going crazy!

**"I said... is y'all feeling this Blood shit???"**

Niggaz started spazzing, punching people in the face and throwing their red flags in the air.

**"That's what's up, because I got something new for y'all! Y'all fools calm the fuck down and listen!"**

Jerry Moore had the homies in a trance! The club got quiet as everybody anticipated the big homies next move.

**"O'kay, now when I say 'Sex'... I want y'all fools to say: 'I wannit!' And when I say 'money'... Y'all say 'gotta have it!' And when I say 'murder'... Y'all say 'always on my**

mind, until the day that I die UBN must shine!'... Y'all fools think y'all can handle that?"

"No doubt, big homie!"

"Get it poppin'!"

"Woof... woof... woof!"

"Let me hear you say, 'sex!'"

"I want it!"

"Money!"

"Gotta have it!"

"Murder!"

"Always on my mind--'

"Hold up! Hold up! Y'all niggaz ain't wit' me! Check it, I'm gonna say this shit myself. When y'all fools feel me, get with the program!"

Jerry Moore put a hand over his face and began to rock back and forth as he chanted the new anthem. He was feeling himself, and by the time he had already said it three times, it was resonating throughout the entire club!

"Sex!"

"I wannit!"

"Money!"
"Got to have it!"
"Murder!!!"
"Always on my mind, til the day that I die, UBN must shine!"
"From this day on, this is what we holla: Sex, Money Murder! Dammit man, shout out to all the fools that rep this set! Blood up!"

Jerry Moore dropped the mic and made his way off the

stage. A-Blood smiled as him and Don Chi-Chi followed the homie through the crowd. New York City was about to be out of control, and this shit wasn't going to be nothing nice.

# Chapter Six

Blueberry-Loc sat up in bed holding his head with both hands. He was leaned over with his elbows on his knees. Ever since the ass beating that left him in a coma, Blueberry-Loc experienced periodic migraines. He would sometimes say that it felt as if a little man was in his head with a sledgehammer swinging it against the walls of his skull like a mad man! Sometimes when the migraines would come, he would get dizzy and his eyesight would become blurred. At times like this, Blueberry-Loc would be on the verge of a panic attack, so he would go to the kitchen or bathroom sink and submerge his head under cold water. Sometimes he would use the tub.

This is how Blueberry-Loc felt right now. His head was hurting so bad he thought he was about to die. He rushed to the bathroom and turned on the cold water, using his hand to cup water to his face. This was one of the reasons he was so set on extracting revenge. He felt he would've been better off if the slobs whom had beaten him into a coma would've just killed him. He was furious that they had left him alive with damaged limbs and organs that no longer worked properly. Most of the time, Blueberry-Loc was miserable, and he felt as if he was dying a thousand deaths as a paralytic.

No one he was close to actually knew the heavy load he was carrying. They didn't know his inner feelings. Had his mother, Mary, or Uncle Ray known the misery that he wallowed in, they could've pointed out all the blessings that he obviously couldn't see. Blueberry-Loc was alive and breathing! This was a blessing by itself. He had all of his senses; his eyesight, his hearing, smell, and tasting. He still had intelligence and understanding. He still had the capacity to feel; happiness, sadness, etc. All of these things were right in front of his face, but he couldn't see it, as if he actually did lose his eyesight. As if he actually was a blind man.

It was 8:30 in the morning, and after Blueberry-Loc had completed his cold water treatment and dried his face off, he studied his appearance in the mirror. His dreads now fell pass his shoulders and they were well groomed. His skin was golden and without blemishes. His sideburns were thin and trimmed low, as was his beard, and his shapeup reminded people of Steve Harvey. Blueberry-Loc had beady eyes, a wide nose, and thick lips. Externally he was handsome, but internally, he felt like shit!

He hobbled into the kitchen and prepared waffles, scrambled eggs with cheese, and turkey bacon. After eating, he fell into his big Lazy-Boy chair in the living room, flicked the plasma to BET, and then grabbed the phone and placed a call to his boy Nasty Nate to be updated on the status of their mission.

Nasty Nate was at the Executive Motel on the south conduit, right off of Rockaway Blvd. He was snoring lightly with a bad caramel complexion chick name Tara cuddled up next to him. He met Tara at the club the night before, she was up in VIP hanging tight with Lashawn and the rest of her girlfriends.

Nasty Nate was a slick dude, and he was respected. He used one of his connects to get a Travagar Square security jacket, and he assigned himself to the VIP section. He was able to observe the animosity brewing between two of his targets and he mentally took note of the chick that his main target had left with.

One step ahead of the game, Nate already peeped that one of Lashawn's girlfriends was all over his nut sack! She kept stealing glances in his direction with a big Kool-Aid smile on her face. He discreetly pushed up on shorty, and when the cat and mouse game was over, the real games began!

Tara had reddish brown hair that was cut short and styled like Toni Braxton's. She had perky small breast, but her ass was something that you just had to see!

Nasty Nate had earned his name honestly, and true to form, once he got Tara inside the hotel room, homeboy got his freak on! He licked her asshole as if it was a soul food platter! Shorty squirmed and sucked in air as he inserted a finger in her rectum and used his tongue to slap box with her clit.

Tara closed her eyes and held his head firmly, and Nate didn't understand why, but it sounded like she was crying. He rubbed his face in her wet pussy and continued to do what he loved to do.

After Tara returned the favor, passionately sucking his balls and running her tongue up and down the length of his dick, Nate decided to test the quality of the Viagra he popped while they were still at the club. His manhood felt harder than a roll of quarters!

He put shorty on all fours and admired her pretty ass wiggling in the air. She had a tattoo of a butterfly on her right ass check, and on the left ass check was a heart with a banner going across that read: Big Steve. Nasty Nate almost laughed out loud as he let the tip of his dick trace the crack of her ass. If he was able to control himself, before the night was over he was going to submerge Big Steve's name in a nice puddle of cum.

When he finally penetrated Tara, her pretty little ass started crying again. At first, Nate was turned on by the sounds she was making, but after a while, he began wondering what the fuck was wrong with shorty.

'*She wanna cry,*' Nate thought to himself, '*I'll give her ass a reason to cry!*'

Nate slid his dick out the pussy and plunged it in shorty's ass! Tara turned around with her mouth wide open in shock.

49

"Oooooooh, damn!!! I thought you'd never get around to this tight ass," she screamed.

Tara was backing that ass up, meeting Nate's thrust! They went at it for hours, fucking and sucking! It was eight in the morning when Nate was finally able to plant his seed all over Tara's left butt check. He fell back on the bed exhausted.

"Ayo," he said before he fell asleep. "Who the hell is Big Steve?"

Tara had no shame in her game. "Oh, that's my baby daddy, he locked up."

'*Bitches ain't shit,*' Nate thought. '*But then again, it ain't her fault that nigga got locked up!*'

"I guess shit don't stop when a nigga get knocked!" he said aloud.

"Hel-lo!" Tara said in agreement, before the two of them fell into a slumber.

Nate was awakened about a half hour later by the sound of airplanes dropping bombs, and the bombs exploding. This was the ring tone he used for Blueberry-Loc, but in his dream, he thought it was a terrorist attack. He snapped awake and sat up in bed looking confused. When it dawned on him that his phone was ringing, he grabbed it and put it to his ear.

"Hello?"

"Nasty Nate, what's crackin'?"

"Ain't shit, boss! What you doing up so early?" Nate called everybody boss.

"It's almost nine o' clock! Don't nothing come to a sleeper but a dream!"

"I JUST went to sleep, cuz," Nate said whining.

"What time are you coming to see me?" Blueberry-Loc was eager to find out what happened.

"Around 1:00."

"I'll see you when you get here."

"Alright boss."

Nate hung up the phone. He lifted up the sheets and watched Tara lying on her stomach. Before he laid back down, he parted her soft ass checks and ran his tongue up the crack of her ass.

Blueberry-Loc was looking out the porch window when the white 350Z Nissan pulled up in front of the crib on shiny chrome rims. He met Nate at the front door, and then they both made their way to the living room.

"Ayo! The party was off the heezy!" Nate said

Blueberry-Loc was the type of person, no matter what somebody said, he would look at them as if they said some serious shit.

"And-" Nate continued, "I think we can kill two dogs with one stone."

"What did you find out?" Blueberry-Loc asked, falling back into his easy chair.

"Well for starters…" Nate said doing a crip dance. "Chandar was at the party."

"What?!?" Blueberry-Loc said in amazement, sitting on the edge of his chair.

"You'll be happy to know that Jerry Moore was just as surprised as you are."

"Why didn't you call me???"

"I was in the middle of a mission. My job was to obtain information."

Blueberry-Loc slammed his fist into the palm of his hand. Chandar was back in New York!

"Jerry Moore is in section 5 of Rochdale as we

speak. If you want, I can go and put that nigga in the dirt. And then we can catch Chandar at the funeral, it'll be like déjà vu." Nasty Nate spoke matter of factly.

"No! We're not gonna kill them yet. That would be mercy. To make a nigga die bleeding is nothing; you make a nigga die breathing, then you saying something.

"Okay boss... So what's your plan?"

"I wanna destroy these niggaz first!" Blueberry-Loc said, and then continued. "I want them to suffer! I wanna take away the things that they love, make 'em miserable! Then I want them to die, and I want them to die slowly!"

Nate looked at Blueberry-Loc and was happy they weren't enemies. Blueberry-Loc was a crazy mother fucker with a black heart.

"That sounds like an excellent plan, boss. Plus I have some more news. Chandar and Jerry Moore was about to fight. They was in a heated argument and Chandar smashed a bottle against the wall. It almost got ugly up in there."

Blueberry-Loc pondered on this last piece of information. This was perfect. Everything was about to come together like butt checks. Jerry Moore and Chandar were finally going to pay for what they did.

"Okay, cuz. I got a plan!"

# Chapter Seven

When Jerry Moore was ten years old and in the fifth grade, his mother made a decision that would alter his life forever. She allowed Jerry to be evaluated and placed into Special Education classes.

The truth was, Jerry was a smart kid. He was far from the brightest, but he definitely couldn't be classified as being slow or stupid. Jerry's problem was that he didn't like to listen. He was always talking in class, being disruptive, and he never did his homework. Jerry Moore was also a bully, but every school has one of those.

What Bernadette Moore couldn't have known was that by allowing her son to be placed in Special Education, he was actually going to be surrounded by other kids that were just like him; bad as hell! Sure, in a smaller class the teachers would be able to keep a closer eye on him, but the fact was, it would be far easier to deal with one Jerry Moore as opposed to dealing with ten kids just like him.

Ms. Bernadette only wanted what was best for her son, but with this situation, she clearly didn't analyze all of her options. Jerry Moore needed someone to talk to him, to explain to him exactly what he was doing wrong, and why it was important for him to straighten up.

Unfortunately, Ms. Bernadette didn't have the

*patience to do this. When she wasn't yelling or screaming at her son, her other remedy was a good old fashion ass whipping. This caused Jerry to rebel! Incorporate with that the fact that Jerry had no male role model, so there was no proper example for him to follow. He didn't even know who or where his father was! The only thing that Bernadette knew about Jerry's father was that they called him Jay-Dub. She was only intimate with him one time when she was seventeen years old. By the time Bernadette had realized she was pregnant, Jay-Dub and his family had moved to Atlanta, Georgia. Only God knew where he was now.*

*It was at open school night that Jerry's teacher, Mrs. Singleton, suggested to Bernadette that Jerry be placed in 'a smaller class'. It may have been suggested with good intentions, but it was an uninformed suggestion nevertheless. Mrs. Singleton didn't have a clue as to what went on in those smaller classes. There was no long list of examples of people who went through Special Education and turned out for the better. There was no proof that Special Education was conducive to stimulating the learning process, or appropriate behavior. In fact, the smaller classes served as a network for bad ass kids! Most of these students were being primed for prison, as they became extortionist, armed robbers, drug dealers, and rebels with a lack of respect for authority. The smaller classes accomplished the goal of making these particular children feel as if they were outcast. They were laughed at and made fun of. The teachers could not control them, so most teachers didn't even try to. The teachers who would try to force the kids to pay attention and learn, were looked at as the enemy and part of the system that outcast them in the first place. As a result, the atmosphere was hostile. There was plenty of yelling and screaming, sometimes a chair would be thrown or a table flipped over.*

*Since he was a child, Jerry Moore was always aggressive. When he wanted something that someone else had, he would take it. When he got upset, instead of trying to express himself, he would fight. He would fight anybody and everybody, except for his mom, and sometimes he even thought about fighting her. In elementary school, he was a big fella for his age, so beating up the other little kids was a piece of cake. It wasn't until junior high school that he first ran into some problems.*

*Jerry Moore was in a class that consisted of twelve people. It was his first day in the seventh grade and the teacher wanted everyone to introduce themselves to the class. In all, it was five girls and seven boys. Distrustful of getting too familiar with total strangers, Jerry Moore was being disruptive.*

*"This is some little kid shit! We did this in first grade. I didn't come here to introduce myself to nobody."*

*The teacher was taken aback, but she was used to this type of behavior by now.*

*"Calm down Mr. Moore, no one is going to force anybody to do anything. I'm just trying to get the class off to a good start."*

*That was fine with Jerry. He just sat at the back of the class room with one of his eyes squinted and the other one wide open, looking crazy! Although he didn't participate, he did manage to memorize almost everyone's name in the class. One guy in particular had a name that Jerry Moore thought was hilarious. Jerry Moore waited until class got a break before approaching the guy to start some trouble.*

*"Hey, Chandelier! What the fuck was your mother drinking when she named you that?"*

*"Who you talking to, money grip," the guy asked looking around mockingly.*

*"I'm talking to you, Chandelier!"*

*"My name is Chandar! Shhhan-dar! You can't possibly be as dumb as you look, so next time, get it right." That's all*

55

*Jerry Moore needed to hear! He charged at Chandar swinging fists like a mad man. Chandar, not a stranger to a good brawl, slid to the side and shoved Jerry Moore in the direction he was charging. This made Jerry Moore furious! Like a mad man, he yelled and charged again, this time Chandar grabbed one of Jerry's swinging arms and used the momentum to fling him around and then to the ground. Jerry Moore was on his feet immediately, and Chandar used a move where he would sweep his foot on the ground with impressive speed and knock his opponent's feet from under him. That quick, Jerry Moore found himself sitting on his ass again!*

*From that day on, Jerry Moore would give Chandar an evil look, but he was smart enough to stay away from him. Ironically enough, Jerry Moore was still a trouble maker, and carried himself with the attitude of a bully.*

*One day, a group of guys from the regular classes were humiliating a nerdy looking guy from Special Ed.*

*"Hey, dum-dum! You're going to have to walk home today because the little yellow school bus left already."*

*"Ah, ha, ha, ha!"*

*"They're all gonna laugh at you... They're all gonna laugh at you."*

*"Ayo... Ayo... Why y'all got more teachers in your class than students?" Everybody in the vicinity was cracking up! One girl, about thirteen years old, tried to defend the poor guy.*

*"Why don't y'all leave him alone, he's not bothering anybody?"*

*"Yeah, why don't we leave the Special Ed. victim alone... Before handyman comes to get us!" The kids exploded with laughter. Out of nowhere, Jerry Moore came swinging balled up fist, pummeling the guy who cracked the last joke.*

*"I'm in Special Ed! Pick on me," he yelled. The guy that Jerry attacked was now on the floor, but two other guys tried to jump on Jerry Moore. Jerry was rumbling with both of them, until Chandar came to even the playing field. Back to back, they fought against all the guys from the regular classes that dared to engage them in battle.*

*The next day, the big fight was the talk of the school. The guys in Special Ed. now had a reputation. Not only would they fight, but they also stuck together. Jerry Moore and Chandar had created a bond, one that would last far longer than either of them could ever have anticipated.*

The big homie was weighing his options. He wasn't waiting for anybody to give him shit! They were in Baisley Projects, building four, on the seventh floor, in Ms. Peaches' apartment. It was Jerry Moore, A-Blood, Don Chi-Chi, G-Bundles, Bugsy, and Tank. They were crowded into the small living room waiting on some very important phone calls. They chose to meet at this particular apartment because Ms. Peaches was cool people, and she was in contact with someone that Jerry Moore needed to speak with. That person was Big Ive.

At one point, Big Ive and his homie Don John had a choke hold on all criminal activity taking place in Baisley Projects. Their careers were ended when the feds came into the picture, and they were ultimately sentenced to football numbers that had to be served in federal prison.

Jerry Moore was seeking approval from Big Ive to open up shop, if need be, and he wanted to make Baisley his headquarters. He was actually doing this out of respect for A-Blood, because Don John and Big Ive were A-Blood's people. Plus, Jerry Moore knew that he would receive more hood cooperation if he had the blessings of Big Ive.

They were also waiting on a phone call from Del Gibson, CEO at Loud Mouth Records. A-Blood was trying to get Jerry Moore a job as an A&R, and Jerry Moore already had an act that he wanted to sign; G-Bundles and Bugsy, two up and coming gangsta rappers.

The last call Jerry Moore was waiting on was from Chuck, the old cocaine supplier that he bumped into at the club. Jerry Moore was exploring all of his options.

"Ayo, Don Chi-Chi," Jerry Moore started. He was leaned back on the couch with his feet kicked up on the coffee table. "What's up with your cousin Cue? If shit pop off, you think he wanna come get some of this money with us in Queens?"

"Of course," Don Chi-Chi said, exhaling haze smoke out the window. Him, G-Bundles, and Bugsy were smoking blunts to the head. Jerry Moore couldn't understand how these dudes could sit around and smoke, smoke, smoke all day. The big homie was use to being around Generals, but these little niggaz was almost like fiends.

A-Blood was in the love seat talking on his cell phone, and Big Tank was leaning against the wall with his arms folded as if he was on security detail. Jerry Moore made a mental note to make sure he kept Tank close to him... Security minded people was sometimes hard to find.

"A-Blood, how your people supposed to get through to you if you're burning up the phone? Dammit man," Jerry Moore said, fucking with the homie. A-Blood shot a look in the big homies direction to see if this nigga was serious. Jerry Moore wore an evil grin.

"I got call waiting, homie. Be easy. Everything is going according to plan."

"It better be," Jerry Moore shot back, and then continued. "G-Bundles, Bugsy, y'all niggaz got enough material to put out

a mix tape while y'all work on your album?"

G-Bundles, AKA Gino, eyes red from the trees, was the first to speak. "I got crazy material! We can probably put out two or three mix tapes while we working on the album. The only thing is, how we gonna do shows, go on tour and shit, when both of us are on the run?"

Jerry Moore had forgot about that. Both Gino and Bugsy had violated parole, and now they were on the run.

"We'll cross that bridge when we get to it. For now, if everything goes as planned, we'll just flood the street with mix tapes. Maybe we'll throw a few talent shows and see what we can find. It's fucked up, all the real talent is either in jail or y'all niggaz is on the run. Dammit man! Ayo, Tank! Why you don't sit your fat ass down and write some raps or something? You on that brainiac shit. I know you better do something around this ma-fucker to earn your stay."

Tank had a silly grin on his face. Jerry Moore knew that Tank was bringing a lot to the table, so he left him alone, and focused on Don Chi-Chi.

"Don Chi-Chi, that's why y'all niggaz is fucked up now! All y'all wanna do is get high. I'm a start calling you Smokey!"

"Naw big homie, it ain't like I'm addicted to this shit. It just be something to do," Don Chi-Chi said, defending himself.

"You want something to do nigga, get money! Fuck y'all niggaz gonna have my back and y'all high all the time? That shit is crazy," Jerry Moore said.

Everybody was quiet. Only thing you heard was A-Blood talking on his cell phone, but A-Blood was aware of everything that was taking place. He sat there with a smirk on his face while Jerry Moore ran his house.

Jerry Moore didn't want to shit on Don Chi-Chi, especially

after the homie displayed complete loyalty at the club. If Don Chi-Chi was willing to put in work on Chandar, Jerry More knew this little nigga had his back for real.

"I fucks witchu hard, Chi-Chi! But y'all niggaz lose focus too quick. Everybody wanna fuck bitches and get high! Everybody wanna spend money! It's about discipline. Y'all niggaz know my track record, I *raise* bosses! Whether we take this shit to the streets or not, it's gonna be a chain of command. As of now, Chi-Chi, you're the number two! You're gonna be my under boss, so I need you to be on point. Is that too heavy for you?"

"Nah big homie, I got you!"

Jerry Moore dug in his pocket and pulled out a knot of money. It was the ten grand that Chuck gave him at the club. Jerry Moore leaned over and put it on the coffee table.

"That's all you, homie," he said watching Chi-Chi closely. Don Chi-Chi's eyes were glued to the money as if he were in a trance. Jerry Moore continued. "That's just for starters. The more money I see, the more money you see. I want you to recruit your cousin Cue, I heard he good with numbers. I want him to come work for me. While Gino and Bugsy is in the studio pushing out mix tapes, we gotta explore our other options. Big Tank is in charge of-"

"Jerry, telephone," Ms. Peaches yelled, interrupting the meeting. Jerry Moore got up and walked into the kitchen, picking up the phone from off the counter.

"Hello?"

"Yeah, what's up?" the voice on the other line barked.

Jerry Moore smirked, "Who's this, Ive?"

"Yeah! My man got word to me that you wanna talk; for obvious reasons this ain't a good way."

"I feel you homie! I just needed your name and number so I can send you some loot." Big Ive was silent on the other end. "I was thinking about moving in with Ms. Peaches for a while and I wanted your blessings." Big Ive understood what this implied.

"Yeah, it's all good! Send that paper out, and make sure you send something to my man, Don John. If you run into any obstacles, tell Peaches, and she'll get word to me. Anything else you wanna contribute to the cause you can give it to A-Blood, and he'll make sure I get it.

"No doubt, I appreciate that! Keep ya head up, Soldier and Stay sucka free!"

"You do the same, and be safe. One!"

"Peace!"

The first part of Jerry Moore's plan for taking it to the streets was almost complete. He left another voice message for Chuck, instructing him to give him a call asap. He had just got comfortable on the sofa when his cell phone rang.

When Chuck's black Acura NSX pulled behind 116-40 Guy R. Brewer Blvd, AKA building four, Ms. Peaches was on her way out. She was going to spend the night in Queens-Bridge with some of her friends.

A-Blood had left about an hour ago. After receiving the call from Del Gibson, and securing a job for Jerry Moore, he departed to meet up with Chandar.

Jerry Moore and his team were up in Ms. Peaches' apartment buggin' out listening to 50 cent's Get Rich or Die Trying CD when someone knocked at the door. Tank stood on the tip of his toes and looked out the peep hole before opening the door for Chuck and leading him into the living room. Don Chi-Chi brought a chair from the dining room and instructed Chuck to have a seat. Jerry Moore silently watched as Chuck entered his interim domain. The big homie had one eye low and one eye high, and there was no sign that he even acknowledged that Chuck had entered the room.

This is the reason why Chuck didn't want to return this nigga's call. The big homie was crazy! Now this nigga had him alone in an apartment that resembled a dungeon, and for some reason, Chuck had a bad feeling. To avoid a situation like this, Chuck had attended the welcome home party thrown for the big homie. He had given the big homie ten thousand dollars and his phone number, out of both respect and fear! Now Chuck's hope was that the big homie would take protection payments in disguise of love, and allow Chuck to humbly exist. His hope was that the big homie wouldn't be too greedy and want it all, because this would inevitably mean Chuck's death and Chuck didn't want to die.

"Big homie, what's good? I tried to get here as quick as I could," Chuck said, trying to mask his fear.

"Who told you to speak," Jerry Moore spat, taking control of the situation.

*'This was bad. This was looking really bad.'* Chuck didn't attempt to say another word, but his mind was racing, thinking of ways to get the hell out of that apartment alive.

"Only speak when you're spoken to. I'm gonna ask the questions, and you're gonna answer them. You understand me?"

"Yes I understand, big homie."

Chuck was being submissive and Jerry Moore loved it! Jerry Moore missed this kind of power with a passion. He had to have it! In a way, he was like a little kid dying for authority just so he could abuse it.

"How come you kept sending my calls to your voicemail?"

*That's why this nigga is going crazy! Damn! I knew I should've answered the first time.'*

"That was my bad, big homie. I was in my lawyers' office. I caught a gun charge a few mouth ago and-"

"Shut up! Shut the fuck up," the big homie yelled, and then continued. "Next time I call you, I don't give a fuck if you're at a funeral, you better answer the phone!"

*'He said, 'next time'… he SAID 'next time', that means he's not gonna kill me!'*

"If there is a next time," Jerry Moore added as if he read his mind.

There was another knock at the door, and Tank disappeared to answer it. Then Tank returned to the living room but he wasn't alone. Jerry Moore had imported a big gun from the mean streets of West Philly, and the name alone was enough to make the hair stand up on the back of the necks of killers. Standing in the living room of that Jamaica, Queens housing apartment, was none other than the infamous, Reggie Ransom!

Reggie Ransom had the most confirmed killings on the east coast! This was the boy they called the Grim Reaper! Jerry Moore met Reggie in U.S.P. CANAAN. Reggie was on the ass end of a 20 year sentence for bank robbery. Reggie Ransom wasn't home for a whole year yet, and he was back to business as usual.

He came into the living room and it was as if his eyes had a mind of their own. They took in everything, even the roach making its way to the ceiling. Reggie said nothing, he just made his way over to the window and peeped out before closing the shades. They were on the 7th floor, but Reggie Ransom didn't want to chance the possibility of someone seeing what was taking place in that apartment.

"Okay Chuck," Jerry Moore began, then continued. "Let's get down to business."

Don Chi-Chi, G-Bundles AKA Gino, Bugsy, and Tank were now reminded of why they were willing to follow Jerry Moore to the end. This nigga was about his business!

"I wanna know where the coke is! I want the money too, but I need a whole lot of coke Chuck, in order to do things I plan to do. If I'm satisfied with the coke that you give me, not only will I allow you to live, but I'll give you back that bullshit ten grand you gave me at the club. I'll have you dropped off at the airport or the Port Authority, and you can go somewhere and see how long YOU can survive off of it! What the fuck did you think I was gonna do with ten thousand dollars? Don't you ever disrespect a Don like that! Where's the mother-fuckin' coke, and where's the money, all of it!"

# Chapter Eight

Chandar was a boss, bottom line! Before he left New York, he actually became the boss of bosses of the underworld after he successfully annihilated the most powerful and ruthless gangsta in the city, William Cook, AKA Big Willie.

The difference between Chandar and Jerry Moore was that Chandar had both charisma, and a classy aura unbecoming of a person raised in the ghetto.

Without Chandar, Jerry Moore was no different than any of the other hoodlums whom robbed and killed just for the thrill of the crime. Still, Chandar couldn't believe that Jerry Moore had the audacity to disrespect his beloved Lisa. Lisa had been a good girl; decent. She stood for what was right, and she was killed unjustly. Jerry Moore knew all of this, yet he disrespected Lisa as she lay in her grave. Chandar was *not* feeling that.

Whenever Chandar was in New York, he reserved a suite on the executive floor at the Holiday Inn by La Guardia airport. The suite had three bedrooms with their own full bathrooms, a kitchen with state of the art utilities, a large dining room with a splashing fountain in the middle and three tables situated around it, a sitting room had a fully loaded wet bar that occupied one entire wall, and there were ficus trees in every room.

Chandar was in the bathroom of the master bedroom preparing for a trip to the cemetery. This trip was no doubt provoked by the slick comment made by Jerry Moore at the club, but Chandar always visited Lisa whenever he was in town. He would take flowers, and sometimes stay hours enjoying the solidarity that he once enjoyed with the mother of his child.

Chandar examined his reflection in the mirror. He was dressed smartly in a cashmere sweater, cotton button down shirt, and a silk tie by Domenico Vacca. He wore pants by Moschino and black velvet Gucci shoes. His hair was neatly braided; six corn rows to the back, and his high yellow complexion and youthful appearance somehow accentuated his solemn expression. It was almost as if he was pouting.

The ghetto star quietly slipped out of the suite, careful not to awaken Wild Blood, and made his way to the garage to retrieve his silver Porsche 911. The 415 horsepower turbo engine assured a quick and easy drive to East Islip, Long Island, where Lisa was buried. Chandar only made one stop on the way, and that was for flowers. When Chandar entered the grounds of the cemetery, he drove carefully and respectable as if he were on holy ground. A few people were paying respects to their loved ones, but Chandar felt as if he was alone. After parking, he walked slowly across the fresh cut lawn until he came to the paved path that would lead him to Lisa's grave.

Both hands deep in his pockets, Chandar bravely approached the place that held meaningful pieces of his life that were abruptly snatched from him. Her tombstone read: *From God we came, and to Him is our final return. Lisa Maria Kelly, 1978-1998, R.I.P.*

Chandar placed the flowers on her grave and humbly lowered his head and closed his eyes.

*How can I... say goodbye... to what we haaaad-* The Boys II Men version of *Its So Hard to Say Goodbye to Yesterday* played in his head.

While Chandar's exterior was hard as a rock, deep down inside he was sensitive. Lisa's death left him feeling empty, and even though she was killed over 3 years ago, Chandar was still deeply affected. While on one hand, he still had an active sex life, on the other, he was afraid of commitment. He was afraid to get too deeply involved with anyone because of the pain associated with loss. Chandar didn't think that he could handle that again.

"Damn... I miss you Lisa," Chandar whispered. Chandar always spoke aloud at Lisa's grave site as if she could actually hear him.

"I miss you and I wish you were here... I'm lonely without you. Every time I look at our baby girl... I feel shame. It feels like she's being cheated... Because she needs you just as much as I do. She's in the 3rd grade now, and she's smart... Just like you. Her mind is agile... She challenges me... Not in a disrespectful way, she does it the same way you use to do it. You know I can't cook for nothing, but Jasmine will say... 'Daddy, you have to learn how to cook... You can't feed me fast food all the time.' Then I would say to her, 'well, why don't you learn how to cook'... and your daughter would say, 'because that's *your* responsibility.' I'm telling you Lisa, you would be proud of her."

"Your mother is doing real good... She's been clean since you left us. And Lucky... Lucky's a writer now, he's a published author. You didn't die in vain, Mami! And... I know you probably wouldn't approve but... I'm still gonna find out who told William Cook where your mother lived, and when I do... They're gonna pay for what happened to you, just like William Cook paid. Whatever is in the dark, will come to the light. Rest in peace my baby... rest in peace."

*Although I taaake... With me these memories... To be my sunshine after the rain... It's so hard... To say goodbye...*

*To yesterday.*

When Chandar was back in his car, the first thing he did was call his daughter. When he heard her voice, a wave of emotions swept through his body.

"Hi, Daddy," she said gleefully.

"Hey, Princess! How you doing?"

"Fine. I was watching cartoons."

"Are your behaving yourself?"

"Yes! Grandma Cynthia said if I be good, she's going to take me to Chuck E. Cheese."

"So you make sure you behave yourself. You know Daddy loves you, right?"

"Yes! I love you too, Daddy! When you coming home?"

"When I finish taking care of business in New York, Princess. I have a surprise for you when I get back too, okay?"

"Ohhhhhhh! What is it Daddy, tell me what it is!"

"Then it won't be a surprise."

"See, so why you tell me? Now I really can't wait for you to come home. I wish you was home right now!"

"Remember what I told you about patience?"

"Yes! Patience is a virtue, and good things come to those who wait."

"That's my baby! I love you with all my heart! Be a good girl and I'll talk to you later, okay?"

"Okay Daddy, call me before I go to sleep."

After Chandar got off the phone with his daughter, he called the little homie Makavelli and told him to get in touch with O' Corleone. There was going to be a meeting later on that night at Chandar's hotel suite. He also contacted A-Blood and gave him that same message. Don Chi-Chi had to be disciplined for his actions, so Chandar was taking the issue to the table.

As he maneuvered the Porsche down the Belt Parkway, the sound of Denise Williams singing *Black Butterfly* was enough to relax the big homie. He'd weathered the storm, and he came up, so he couldn't let this situation with Jerry Moore nor Don Chi-Chi pull him back into his old ways. Simultaneously, he couldn't just ignore what happened, but he also knew that diplomacy was a must. Don Chi-Chi was still his little homie, but Chandar didn't underestimate anybody! In the words of Jim Hightower, "Even a little dog can piss on a big building."

Chandar made his way to the first lane so he could make the right turn onto the Van Wyck Expressway. His stomach was growling, so he was on his way to Karen's Soul Food Restaurant.

On Queen's Boulevard, he found a parking spot in front of an eggshell white Cadillac Escalade. Inside the restaurant Chandar was greeted by the smell of fried chicken, macaroni and cheese, buttery biscuits and apple pie. The glass counter was situated so customers could see all the food, and it was easy for the plates to be made as you went through the line.

A Jennifer Lopez replica approached Chandar with a friendly smile.

"Do you see anything you like," she asked innocently.

"Is that a trick question," Chandar responded playfully. Baby girl was confused at first, but she finally caught on.

"Oh my God, I mean, are you ready to order! I had no idea how ambiguous that question was."

"That's cool, Mami. I knew what you meant, I was just messing with you. Give me an order of peas and rice… Some macaroni and cheese, what's that right there, oxtails?"

"Yes, and they are delicious."

"Chandar?!?" A female voice interrupted. Chandar turned to his right and was taken aback by the face that went with the voice. It had been about six months since he saw Karen, but he didn't recall her looking so lovely.

"My, my, my, little sis, long time no see," Chandar said, his words flowing off his tongue like music.

"Don't give me that little sister shit, come give me a hug and stop flirting with Rosa and her dizzy ass. Trust me, she is not in your league."

Chandar couldn't suppress a smile. He looked at Rosa and said, "give me an order of those oxtails, and bring me a Ginger Ale." He winked at shorty, and accommodated Karen with a smothering hug. Karen was smelling like N.T.B. by Victoria Secret. Chandar inhaled deeply, enjoying the smell immensely.

"Where's your road dawg, Jerry Moore? I know that's what brought that ass to New York. I heard he had a party but I was too tired to go, Man. My Aunt Felecia had died and I went to her funeral, after that we had a family get together."

"Sorry about your aunt, Yo!"

"Thank you, but I'm okay. Let's change the subject. Look at you, you look good."

"Don't start! Where's your husband at?"

"You know I'm not involved with anyone. I'm married to my work, Chandar. Niggaz play too many games."

"Kids play to many games, we gotta find you a man."

70

"I don't have time for a man, my work keeps me busy. Speaking of work, how's your club doing?"

"Why don't you fly back with me and find out?" Chandar always flirted with Karen, but that comment just slipped out. Rosa brought Chandar's plate of food and a glass of Ginger Ale, and placed it on the table.

"Thank you, sweetheart," Chandar said as he sat at the table, and then continued. "Don't just stand there with your mouth open, sit down."

Karen sat her curvaceous ass down across from Chandar.

"Why can't you just tell me how it's doing and save me a trip," she said smiling.

*'Damn, shorty is beautiful! I can't believe I'm just noticing it.'*

"Okay, you win. The club is doing great. I enjoy what I do; my work is interesting. I get to meet people from all over the world. Why don't you fly back with me and chill for a week or two. You could use a vacation." On the low, Karen always had a crush on Chandar, but it felt as if he never even noticed her. She couldn't believe he was inviting her to Las Vegas to chill with him.

"Are you serious?"

"If your answer is 'yes', But if your answer is 'no', then nah, I'm just kidding."

"I have to think about it, Chandar. I can't just up and leave, I have a business to run,"

"I'm not leaving until Monday, so you have 2 days to think about it. I'm sure you can make arrangements. Matter of fact-" Chandar pushed his plate away and stood up. "We can finish this conversation later. You're hanging out with me tonight. I'm cooking dinner for you. I'm at the Holiday Inn, my usual. Be there by nine o' clock." Karen was stuck. Chandar put a hundred dollar bill on the table. "Don't be late," he said, without waiting for a response. He just gangsta strolled out of the restaurant.

# Chapter Nine

The streets of Jamaica, Queens, was crazy at night! Crack heads was out at an all-time high, going on missions. Stick-up kids were scheming on their next victims. Thug ass niggaz were on the corner getting drunk. And at one point or another, somebody was letting their gun bust!

On 116th Avenue and Supthin Boulvard, Big Time was feeling himself for-real! Today he had copped 125 grams of cocaine. He never had that much coke in his life, but two days ago that changed when his brother was arrested for attempted murder. While Big Time was in his brother's room rummaging through his stuff, looking for some weed, he stumbled across the shoe box containing two thousand dollars.

*Jameek won't be needing this*, Big Time thought as he took the shoe box to his own room.

Big Time planned on taking the train uptown to cop an ounce of coke, his usual. At first he only had eight hundred dollars, but with the discovery of Jameek's stash, he was able to take a cab uptown, and he copped his first big eighth.

Baby boy was on 145th street and Broadway stunting! You couldn't tell that boy he wasn't a boss! He had the cab on hold while he went and checked his man Cheecho. Cheecho was a Dominican dude who could get you whatever you wanted: from a gram to a kilo. He was use to Big Time coming to cop between seven grams and an ounce, but today he was genuinely surprised.

"Papi, you come very big today," he said consulting his calculator watch.

"Well, ya-know ... they can't keep the kid down for long," Big Time responded.

"I give you something extra, okay? I want to see you do good." And that's how that went down. Big Time felt like he was the mayor!

"You hear me son," he said to his partner, Kool-Aid, while they were cooking the cocaine into crack. "We don't have to break this down, we can sell weight!"

Big Time was a funny ass nigga, but he was dead serious. The truth was, if he really wanted to, he *could* supply all the little niggaz on the block who was only interested in buying one or two grams, a half an ounce at the most.

Kool-Aid said, "Nah son, we gonna bag this shit up and flood the block with nickels so we can double our money."

"How about this, son... We bag half up in nickels to put on the block, and with the other half I can sell weight." Big Time wanted to sell weight badder than a ma-fucker, if for no other reason than to tell people he was selling weight. Kool-Aid knew what his boy was up to, so he went ahead and gave him his blessings. As long as he got half, he didn't care what Big Time did. They left the house with the understanding that they would pool the money together when it was time to re-up on the product.

Now Big Time was on The Bully letting everybody know he had it going on. All the hustlers called the Boulevard 'The Bully', and as Big Time watched, Kool-Aid was on his grind getting rid of his half of the work. Big Time was cooler than a Malibu sea breeze. He had already sold three grams of crack at thirty dollars apiece, and Peanut told him he'd be right back with three hundred dollars ... He wanted his ten grams!

"That's what the fuck I'm talking about," Big Time proclaimed. He was in front of Feasters; a mom & pop grocery store/delicatessen.

A couple of kids were off to the side in a heated dice game. Kool-Aid dipped inside the store to make a sell, even though Ms. Debbie and Mr. Willie, the owners, had warned him about making sells in the store. While this was going on, black ass Ebony, a crack head who somehow managed to maintain a healthy fat ass, ran down on Big Time.

"Daddy, can I get something on credit? I just came out and I'm on 'E' ... But once I get motivated, you know I'm gonna bring you some customers."

"Damn Ebony, that ass is still fat as shit! Come 'ere and let me palm that ass. You gotta stop callin' me Daddy out here too." Ebony came closer and turned around so Big Time could fondle her ass.

"I'm sorry Daddy Big Time, but I just needed something to get me started," she whined in a childlike voice.

"I don't have nothing anymore, Yo! I'm selling weight now. You gotta go see Kool-Aid," Big Time said puffed up with pride.

"Where he at?"

"He inside the store."

"You gonna tell him to give me one???"

Big Time was a frontin' ass nigga, but he had a good heart. "Yea, Ebony. Tell him I said to give you one. I'll give you a chance to work that off later."

And Ebony was gone. As she left, Peanut was coming

around the corner. He gave Big Time some dap; at the same time passing him $300.

"Ayo, let me get an extra gram on the house."

Big Time counted the money and made sure it was right.

"I can't do that right now, Nut. I'm just starting out. Wait here, I'll be right back." Big Time went up the block to his crib. He had spent a hundred dollars on a small digital scale. He turned it on and started putting rocks on it until the scale read ten grams, and then he kept snatching small rocks back off until the scale read nine point eight grams. Satisfied, he put the nine-plus grams in a small sandwich bag and made his way back to The Bully.

When he walked on the set, Ebony was waiting on him, along with Peanut and Kool-Aid standing in front of the store.

"Daddy, he won't give it to me," Ebony said accusingly.

"Hold up, Ebony! I'm tryin' to take care of business," Big Time said as he passed Peanut the sandwich bag of crack.

"Big Time, you gotta step ya game up," Peanut said and then continued. "That nigga Chuck always give us extra when we cop from him."

"Chill nigga, I did give you extra," Big Time lied. Peanut held the bag up and examined the contents.

"Oh word? Good looking, kid!"

"Nigga put that shit away, that shit ain't legal," Kool-Aid yelled. He was mad because Peanut was making the spot hot, but he was really upset because Big Time wanted him to give crack head Ebony something for free.

As if Big Time could read his mind, he said, "Yo, Kool-Aid! Give Ebony one of them things, I got you." Kool-Aid gave Big Time an evil look, but he did what he was told.

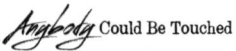 

"Thank you, Daddy," Ebony said to Big Time.

"I told you stop calling me Daddy!"

"Okay Daddy Big Time," Ebony said happily, before jetting off to smoke her crack.

"You act like you really like that bitch," Kool-Aid said with an attitude.

"Naw son," Big Time said, pulling out his cell phone before continuing, "I met this bad chocolate chick on the Avenue the other day. That's who I really like." Big Time dialed her number and someone answered on the second ring.

"Hello, can I speak to Yvette?"

There were three guys inside the house. G-Bundles was using duct tape to bound their hands and legs, while Don Chi-Chi stood nearby with the chrome four fifth aimed at the ground.

"Put tape over their eyes and mouth too," Don Chi-Chi instructed and then continued, "Except for him; I need him to see what's going on," he said, pointing to one of the dudes that was crying.

Chuck had told them he had fourteen kilos of cocaine there, but these guys were claiming that there was only four.

After G-Bundles was sure that the three guys were securely taped, he began going on a rampage in the house looking for anything of value. He took jewelry, weed, and he found a dresser drawer full of cash, but the rest of the coke was nowhere to be found.

G-Bundles dumped all the valuables inside a pillowcase off one of the beds, probably Chuck's. He put a few pieces of jewelry and some cash in his pocket for self, and then went back downstairs where Don Chi-Chi was patiently waiting with the victims.

"What's that," he asked as Gino approached.

"This ain't it," G-Bundles said, dropping the pillowcase and sending a barrage of punches to the face of the victim that was watching his every move.

"Aaar, stop! Help me," the victim was yelling. Gino smothered a hand over his mouth.

"Shut the fuck up before I kill you. Where the coke at? If you start yelling again, I swear to God, I'll cut your tongue out your mouth! You understand?" The guy shook his head up and down real fast; he was scared to death. One of the guys was sitting in a puddle and the smell of urine and feces was in the air. Gino took his hand away from his mouth.

"Where's the coke at?" The guy could barely speak.

"I... I... pleeeeease!" And he was crying again. Gino had a look like he was about to do something drastic... Don Chi-Chi interceded. He bent down next to the guy.

"Listen shorty, calm down. I don't know you, and truthfully, I don't wanna see you get hurt, okay?" The guy was looking at Chi-Chi, nodding his head. He wanted to trust somebody, and he didn't want to die. "I need you to calm down," Chi-Chi continued. "And I need you to tell me where that coke is."

Shorty found his voice. "I don't know where it's at. If I did, I swear, I would've told y'all by now. It was only four." Don Chi-Chi was watching shorty closely. The look in Shorty's eyes said he was telling the truth and Chi-Chi believed him. He stood up and pulled out his cell phone and dialed a number.

"Yo, that nigga lied, he only got four of them things here," said Chi-Chi to Jerry Moore. "Alright... Naw, I don't know... He right here... Alright... Alright, bet," said Chi-Chi

78

and hung up the phone.

"What he say," Gino asked.

"He's sending Reggie Ransom." Don Chi-Chi paced back and forth, looking out the front window every now and then, while G-Bundles continued the search.

A full half an hour had passed before Reggie Ransom arrived. Don Chi-Chi let him in through the side door. G-Bundles came downstairs empty handed.

"Y'all still didn't find it," Reggie asked looking at Gino.

"Uh um!"

"Well, the boy said these kids know where it's at. He said it was all together." Reggie Ransom looked at the three guys taped up, sitting on the floor. He went to find something that would help him send his message… He came back with a hammer.

"Road dawg," he said, directing his speech at shorty whose eyes wasn't covered. "Listen to me, make it easy on yourself. You're in a lot of trouble. Tell me where it's at, so we can get up out of here." Baby boy was scared back into silence. He wanted to say something, but he couldn't find the voice. He was sure he was going to die anyway, so he didn't want to tell them shit.

Reggie Ransom gave him a few seconds to respond, and then he said, "You don't hear me though, huh?!?" He played eeny meeny miney moe with the other two victims, and when he stopped, he looked at shorty one more time before smashing the hammer into one of the other guy's heads. Blood squirted everywhere and the hammer got stuck in the guy's head. Reggie yanked it out and hit the guy again. As soon as shorty started screaming like a bitch, Gino smothered his mouth with his hand again. The other blindfolded guy was shifting his body around now, trying to get loose.

Reggie Ransom wiped the blood from the hammer off on his pants leg. He looked at shorty and went to find the stereo. He found it and turned on the radio. He found a station playing hip-hop and put that joint on full blast. He walked back over to shorty and instructed Gino to let him go. Shorty started screaming again, but he was being drowned out by the music.

Reggie Ransom yelled over the music. "Ain't nobody gonna hear you, road dawg. Now where it's at?"

Shorty kept screaming and Reggie took the hammer and bashed the next guy in the face. He was in a frenzy, and he wouldn't stop. Blood was everywhere now, and two people were dead. Reggie Ransom was ready to get it over with and just kill shorty so they could get up out of there. But when he looked over at shorty, the little dude was yelling, 'Okay'. Reggie read his lips.

"What's that, road dawg," asked Reggie, bending down so he could hear more clearly.

"They're outside in my car! They're outside in my car!"

"Where at," Reggie yelled at him.

"They're in the trunk!"

"Where's the keys at, and what kind or car am I looking for?"

"It's the only one in the driveway and the keys are in my pocket."

"Alright, thanks!" Reggie Ransom said before he buried the hammer into Shorty's forehead. He left it there while he went through shorty's pocket and found the car keys.

"Tss! Kids," said Reggie and shook his head as he went to check the car. The mission was over.

# Chapter Ten

O' Corleone and Makavelli the Don were the last ones to arrive for the meeting. When they walked into the suite, Wild Blood was playing Xbox on the big screen TV, and A-Blood was on the phone, that was his regular. Chandar came from out the back looking like he just finished working out. His body was toned and he was rocking a white wife beater with some 'E.C.' blue jean shorts. He wore crisp white on white Air Force 1's, and a platinum teddy bear, shrouded with diamonds, swung from a 26 inch platinum chain.

"AH, AHH, AHHH!!! Wild Blood, look who's here fool," Chandar yelled. Wild Blood looked up from his game.

"Lucky, what's poppin'," he said with a smirk.

"Who's Lucky," Makavelli asked in mock confusion.

"Oh yeah, my bad! Makavelli the Don, what's poppin'?"

"Do not get this nigga started," Corleone said, looking at Makavelli with a smirk.

"Do I sense hate in the air," Makavelli asked as he brushed his shoulders off. Makavelli went over and embraced Chandar, then gave Wild Blood some dap, and O' Corleone followed suit.

"Y'all niggaz making all that noise while a nigga on the jack," A-Blood said as he hung up the phone and placed it on his hip, and then continued. "O' Corleone, AKA Seventeen,

Makavelli the Don, AKA that nigga that faked his own death...
What the fuck is up?"

"What da deally, A-Blood," Makavelli said with a warm
smile.

"AKA Phone Jones," Corleone added, and everyone
started laughing.

"Ayo, A-Blood... I know where Makavelli got his AKA
from, but what's up with that Seventeen shit, playa," Chandar
asked.

"Tell 'em Corleone," A-Blood said laughing.

"That shit ain't funny dawg, you tell him," Corleone shot
back. Everybody watched A-Blood, waiting for the explanation.

"That nigga got seventeen confirmed killings under his
belt," A-Blood said as a matter of fact. The room was silent for
a few seconds. No man in that suite was a stranger to murder.
O' Corleone and Makavelli, AKA Lucky, were the ones who
kidnapped William Cook's wife, Michelle, which in turn
triggered the counter-kidnapping of Lucky's mother and sister,
Lisa. That single incident resulted in O' Corleone's brother,
Dave, being killed, along with Makavelli's sister, Lisa, who was
also Chandar's baby's mother.

Someone had told William Cook where Makavelli lived,
and as fate would have it, his mother and sister were both home
when the goons came calling. To this day, nobody knew who
betrayed them, but William Cook hinted to Makavelli that it was
one of his Blood homies. Chandar had put up a $50,000 reward
for anyone who had that information, but had yet to learn the
truth.

"If y'all niggaz want something to drink, get it now so
we can start this meeting," Chandar said, getting the ball rolling,
and then continued. "Cause at 9:00, I need y'all to be ghost. I got

things to take care of."

Makavelli didn't need to be told twice. He made himself some Hennessey and coke before getting comfortable on the love seat. O' Corleone sat on one of the stools by the bar. When Chandar saw that everyone was settled down, and he had their attention, he painted a picture of what took place at the club. He didn't go into detail about the conversation he had with Jerry Moore, but he highlighted the action of Don Chi-Chi. When Chandar was done speaking, he posed a question. "How do y'all think we should deal with this?"

A-Blood wanted to see how the other homies felt before he stated his opinion, so he was on fall-back status. Makavelli had a look of disbelief on his face and he was the first to speak.

"Fuck was the homie thinking? That shit is crazy, dawg! If it went down the way you explained it, then Don Chi-Chi is in serious violation."

"I brought that nigga home..." Corleone started and then continued. "It probably ain't nobody in this room who love the dawg more than I do, but... Make the call, homie. It's your call. I'm going with whatever you say." This is why Chandar fucked with these niggaz... Loyalty!

"If you pick up a starving dog and make him prosperous, he will not bite you. That is the difference between dog and man," Chandar said, quoting Mark Twain.

"If it was up to me, I'd push that nigga shit back," Wild Blood stated angrily.

"That's one suggestion," Chandar said.

"You hear me, fool," A-Blood interjected, directing his speech toward Chandar. "Don Chi-Chi is in violation, ain't nobody in this room gonna argue that. But for two reasons I don't think we should merk shorty... Actually, it's three reasons.

One, that nigga was one of the homies who ran up in the funeral home and put some heavy duty work in on William Cook. Two, that's Jerry Moore's little man. The homie gonna feel some way if we take it to that extreme… And three, we have a long list of other remedies we can use to teach the little homie a lesson."

"Like what? Cut his hands off," Chandar asked sarcastically.

"It's your call, one way or the other, big homie," Corleone said, and then continued. "Like I said, Don Chi-Chi is my dawg; and A-Blood has a point. The little nigga put in some work for the home team, so I really don't wish death on the little homie. Nevertheless, if you give the word, y'all can change my AKA to Eighteen." The room was silent. Everyone understood that O' Corleone was volunteering to slump his homie, if need be. Chandar meditated on all that was said.

"A-Blood! I'm giving that little nigga a pass, but I want you to charge that nigga hard. Let that fool know you saved his life playboy, and he better stay the fuck out my way, bottom line! Tell Jerry Moore I need to be back in Nevada by Monday, so make sure that nigga come see me. Tell him don't make me come looking for him neither. Its ten minutes to nine, y'all niggaz gotta get the fuck out of here. I'll get up with y'all tomorrow." Chandar said the last part with a smile on his face. All the homies gave that nigga some love and then they were gone.

Chandar made his way to the kitchen to heat up the food, and prepare for a long night with Karen, Shit was about to go down!

# Chapter Eleven

The studios and office of Del Gibson, chief executive officer at Loud Mouth Records, was located at the Soul Convention on Merrick Boulevard.

Del Gibson was the Suge Knight of the east coast! He was a man with a driven personality, and he seldom let anyone or anything get in his way. Artist' and producers alike walked on eggshells around him, because everyone knew, if Del Gibson didn't get what he wanted… There was a problem. If he felt slighted in any way… There was a problem. If he *thought* he was slighted or disrespected… There was a problem!

Woe to him who was unfortunate enough to be on his bad side, and even more so for his adversaries.

However, Del Gibson's motto was, 'Luv is luv, hate is hate.' And in his own words, "How you give it, I return it tenfold!" So if you were on his good side, everything was lovely.

Official dudes and genuine good people got along just fine with Mr. Gibson, and this was the case with Jerry Moore.

Simoya, the receptionist, had buzzed Jerry Moore and Don Chi-Chi into 'The Dungeon', that was what the artists and producers called the studios at Loud Mouth Records. They were directed down a corridor and past a room that contained exercise equipment, and another room that held a soda machine and a microwave. There were also a few guys in a sitting room lounging around a big flat screen TV playing video games. A session was taking place in one of the studios. And then in a large room, at the end of the corridor, is where they found Del Gibson, AKA Doctor Hyde.

As Jerry Moore and Don Chi-Chi entered the room, they analyzed the scenario. There was a pool table in the middle of the room and Del was chalking up his cue tip prepared to take a shot. Three guys stood around laughing and joking as the CEO talked plenty of shit before he took what was potentially the last shot that would end the game.

"Someone please call 9-1-1, eight ball in the corner pocket."

Del Gibson took a soft shot, tapping the eight ball, and then watching as it slowly made its way to the corner pocket and dropped in.

"Vinnie, you better quit while you're ahead, man. You gonna mess around and be doing dead cocka roaches all day." Del said, letting out a burst of laughter.

Vinnie Garrett, the manager of Willie Black and the 4-1-0 Hustlers, laid on his back on the floor with his legs and hands in the air, doing his best imitation of a dead roach. Everyone in the room fell out laughing.

Del Gibson turned his attention to the visitors at the door. The scowl on his face was enough to put Ice Cube to shame.

"Which one of y'all niggaz is Jerry Moore?"

One of Jerry Moore's eyes dipped low, as the other one rose. He felt as if he was being challenged.

"Death to all those who go against me," was his response.

"Excuse me," Del Gibson said, not sure he heard him correctly.

"Yeah, I be that nigga for real. Death to all those who go against me!!!" His statement caught Dr. Hyde off guard, and an uncomfortable silence followed. Everyone in the room was looking at Jerry Moore and Don Chi-Chi as if some serious shit was about to jump off.

Never breaking eye contact, Del Gibson grabbed the chalk and polished the tip of his stick again. His scowl slowly transformed into a smile. "You up for a game of pool, big homie."

Jerry Moore relaxed and offered a smile of his own. "No doubt, but I ain't with the dead cocka roach shit!"

Everybody in the room was laughing again. Del Gibson explained to Jerry Moore that A-Blood was just like his own flesh and blood.

"Any friend of A-Blood is definitely a friend of mine," was the way he put it. They shot pool and kicked it for an hour and a half before Simoya came over the intercom.

"Mr. Gibson... Maxwell Smart is in the reception area."

Maxwell Smart was an up and coming producer that Del employed, but Maxwell wasn't too smart. The guy was under an exclusive contract with Loud Mouth, yet he was constantly selling tracks to rival labels to make money on the side.

Del Gibson walked to the intercom on the wall and pushed a button.

"Send that nigga in," he growled.

Del Gibson had a split personality, He was like Doctor Jekyll and Mr. Hyde, hence he earned the moniker, Doctor Hyde. This guy's mood would change like models on the runway. He wore his signature scowl as he took and missed a difficult shot. His mind was obviously not on the game anymore.

Jerry Moore was planning his next shot when Maxwell

Smart walked through the door.

"What's up, fellas," he said in an upbeat tone, as if everything was all love.

"You hear this nigga," Doctor Hyde asked no one in particular, and then continued. "He wanna know what's up. You tell me what the fuck is up! I thought I told you about trying to make money on the side. You still selling these bitch ass niggaz good music that I have exclusive rights to? You think you got all the fucking sense!"

Maxwell frowned up his face as if he was confused. "Why you trippin', boss man. I got enough music for everybody."

Del Gibson was on his way around the table.

"Why I'm trippin'?" he asked.

The pool stick was already flying through the air!

**Crack!** The stick broke over Maxwell Smart's head and Maxwell fell to the ground. He was discombobulated! Jerry Moore was on automatic. He followed up with another whack, cracking his stick over dudes head. Del Gibson suppressed a smile. He mentally admired Jerry Moore's style. Even though they just met, it was like they were on the same page. Jerry Moore was a street dude, and that was exactly the kind of guy Del Gibson needed on his team.

"Vinnie, help this piece of shit up, and get him cleaned up. That was your last warning Max!"

Doctor Hyde delivered a swift kick to Maxwell's ass before departing, then he was barking orders into his Nextel.

"Sabrina, bring the car around!"

A few seconds later his phone chirped.

"I'm there in 2 minutes," a female voice responded.

After making sure everything was copacetic in studio 'A', Del Gibson, Jerry Moore, and Don Chi-Chi breezed through the corridors of the Soul Convection. Del Gibson was a loner, but by the time he made it outside, his entourage consisted of twelve people. Everyone was rushing to their vehicles.

Sabrina, a cinnamon complexion cutie who was Del's personal driver, had the 62' Maybach gassed up and ready to roll. Del and Jerry Moore slid into the back seat, and Don Chi-Chi sat up front with Shorty.

"Brina, take us to Pasta Lovers on Queens Boulevard," Del said and then continued. "And play that *All Eyes on Me* CD. I feel like hearing some Pac."

*'I won't deny it, I'm a straight rider, you don't wanna fuck with me-'*

They were laid back in the Maybach, listening to *Ambitions of a Rider*, cruising down Merrick Boulevard. There were two S500's, a Seven Forty-Five, a Lincoln Navigator, and a Yukon Denali in their convoy. Jerry Moore was somewhat use to this kind of shine, but he constantly reminded himself that he wasn't the captain of this ship.

He recognized that Del Gibson was a real nigga, and he wanted to explore the possibilities of putting out a few groups, but... And there was always a *'but'* when it came to Jerry Moore... by no means was he willing to accept being a co-captain. With Jerry Moore, it was all or nothing. His days of being a co-captain were over!

After they ate lunch, Del Gibson surprised Jerry Moore by making a trip to the Mercedes Benz dealership. He did this upon request of A-Blood.

"You home now, nigga," Del said as they entered the showroom floor, and then continued. "You may as well step ya shit all the way up!"

There were Benzes lined up, all shapes, colors, and sizes. Jerry Moore walked past the E-Classes and found the big boys. A sale representative quickly came to assist them.

"Good afternoon, gentlemen. My name is Skip, how may I help you?"

Del Gibson transformed into Doctor Hyde.

"For starters, you can go find your boss for me, Skippy! Inform him that Del Gibson is here. After that, be a good kid and bring me a Pepsi."

Skip's face turned red, and he hurried off to find his boss. Mr. Kopell came out of his office and approached Del.

"Mr. Gibson, glad you could make it. Come right this way." While they headed toward the lot, skip rushed up to Del and gave him a cold Pepsi as was requested. Money talk, bullshit walk, was the jewel of the day.

Mr. Kopell led them outside to a fleet of top of the line Benzes. Jerry Moore inspected the CL500, and the SL600, but he wasn't really in the mood for a coupe. He looked over the S-Classes, and then finally set his eyes on the vehicle that he wanted.

"Dammit man! Don Chi-Chi, what you think about this?"

Don Chi-Chi examined the whip Jerry Moore was talking about.

"That shit is bigger than a ma-fucker!"

"This is the DUB Executive stretch K500 Mercedes Benz," Mr. Kopell explained, and then continued. "It's all the luxuries of a Maybach, at half the price. Recliners in the back, three 16 inch monitors, and plenty of wood in the dash."

"You like that homie," Del asked, looking at Jerry Moore.

"It looks like a S-Class," Jerry Moore responded.

"It is an S-Class," Mr. Kopell interjected.

"Yea, I gotta have that!" Jerry Moore decided.

"Put some temporary plates on that, and give my man the keys!" Doctor Hyde said and then continued. "Let's go fill out this paperwork so we can be out."

"I'm afraid the K500 won't be ready to drive off the lot for at least a month, Mr. Gibson. I apologize but ..."

"But nothing! You have two weeks, the latest! Now what do you have available for my man to drive until he can pick up his car," Doctor Hyde yelled.

"Well I can certainly accommodate him with a regular S-Class until then, if that will please you."

"Just give me a white 600, and that should hold me down for now," Jerry Moore said.

"I'm sure you will find the S500 much lighter and easier to handle ..."

"Mr. Kopell, get my man the 600 like he asked for, and let me fill out this paperwork! Time is money," Doctor Hyde roared.

"Right away, Sir," Mr. Kopell complied.

And Jerry Moore drove a white S600 straight off the lot! Del Gibson had some important meetings to attend, so he and Jerry Moore agreed to go separate ways, but they made plans to meet at the Soul Convention the following day.

Jerry Moore had fourteen kilos of cocaine and over a hundred and fifty grand in cash. The person responsible for this good fortune would probably find his face on the side of a milk carton in the days that followed. His name would constantly be on the tongues of the people, mostly in hushed tones, as people wondered, what the fuck happened to Chuck?

Jerry Moore wanted to focus on putting out his first mixtape, but the first order of business was getting rid of all that coke.

He and Don Chi-Chi drove to Guy R. Brewer Boulevard and 112th Avenue. Word on the street was that 112 was a gold mine! The twins, Teddy and Eddie, sold nickels of crack, and a kid name Gee was selling weight. Jerry Moore parked a block away and watched the hustle and bustle of the block. It was still early in the day, but it was clear that money was coming through. Next, they drove to Linden Boulevard and 157th Avenue and conducted similar surveillance. Shit wasn't jumping like 112th, but the block definitely had potential. When Jerry Moore drove to Supthin Boulevard, his mind was made up… The boulevard was flooded with crack fiends! The Bully was like a whole new world. Crack heads were selling TV's, CD players, and anything of value that they could get there filthy hands on. Female fiends stood on corners, prostituting their bodies in exchange for the quick high afforded by crack cocaine. Dealers of death were everywhere, pushing destruction to those whom spirits were broken.

Jerry Moore saw an opportunity to get rich quickly, he just needed to put together the right team. With the right team, getting rid of twenty-eight pounds of cocaine would be a piece of cake.

He drove to Denise's basement apartment and picked up the knapsack containing the 40-grand that A-Blood had gave him. He then navigated the Benz to a used car lot on Hillside Avenue. He copped Don Chi-Chi a gold Lexus GS400. The car had 33,000 miles on it, and the dealer wanted 22 grand.

Jerry Moore talked him down to 20 grand, but gave the man an extra 5 grand in cash to fix the payment plan in a way that the IRS wouldn't notice such a big transaction. The greedy dealer quickly tuned the car up and slapped some temporary plates in the window, then congratulated Don Chi-Chi on his new car. That day was a good day for the dealer… Jerry Moore gave him 25 grand in cash, but he recorded the sale of the Lexus at the price of $18,000.

"What you about to get into," Jerry Moore asked Don Chi-Chi, giving him an opportunity to go floss his new whip. Don Chi-Chi was happier than a young black author signing the contract for his or her first book deal.

"I don't know, Big homie! I'll probably go and check my cousin Cue. After that, I wanna go get my son and take him shopping."

"You got enough money?"

"Yeah, yeah! I still got the ten grand you gave me."

"Alright, meet me in Baisley at nine o' clock, down the hill from building 3. Bring your cousin Cue with you, ya heard!?!"

"Yeah, yeah! I love you, Big homie!" Don Chi-Chi gave Jerry Moore a hug.

"I love you back, fool! Be safe!"

They jumped in their whips and peeled off.

# Chapter Twelve

When Karen entered the suite, Chandar put a finger to his lips indicating that he wanted her to remain quiet. He then grabbed her by the hand and led her into the dining room. Karen relinquished her cell phone and Chandar sent all her calls to voicemail.

Mary J Blige could be heard singing throughout the suite...

*'If you look in my eyes, could you see what I see... la da da da da...'*

Marys' voice incorporated with the sound of water falling from the splashing fountain created a tranquil atmosphere.

One of the glass tables situated around the fountain was beautifully set, and a burning candle was placed in the middle. Karen was flabbergasted! She had never seen this side of Chandar, this was like a dream come true. For years, Karen had harbored her feelings for this man. Sometimes his presence alone was enough to make her panties wet. She had visions of Chandar passionately making love to her, and now, for reasons she was unaware of, her knight in shining armor was coming to take her away.

Chandar pulled out a chair and Karen sat down.

*'My life, my life, my life, my life, my life...'*

The night proceeded like something out of a fairy tale. Chandar had prepared broiled lamb chops sautéed with mushrooms and onions, yellow rice, and broccoli fried with garlic and oil. A red wine was served with the meal.

No words were spoken, but there was heavy eye contact, and occasionally Chandar would bless Karen with a beautiful smile.

When dinner was over, Chandar removed the dirty dishes and retuned shortly with a small strawberry cheesecake that he made from scratch. He fed Karen as if she were a baby.

This whole evening was blowing Karen's mind, and she wanted nothing else than for Chandar to fuck the shit out of her. She wanted to give herself to him totally, because she knew him. Chandar wasn't a man who played games. In a way, the two of them were so alike. Chandar stayed on his grizzy, and Karen was married to her business. After Lisa, Chandar refused to be too involved ... Karen had no time for commitment. Chandar didn't trust people outside his circle ... Karen didn't *deal* with people outside her circle. But deep down, they both had good hearts, and they both wanted to find love.

Chandar took a sip of wine... This was a statement in itself, because Chandar wasn't a drinker, but tonight was special. The big homie stood up, his insides were warm. He disappeared into the back and returned with a black comforter that he spread across the floor near the splashing fountain. He squatted down by Karen and removed her shoes. She was captivated as he massaged her bare feet, and she thanked God she bathed for an hour before she came over. Her feet were lovely, toes painted light sky blue with white tips. Chandar stood up and grabbed her by her hands, helping her to her feet, and gently guided her to the comforter.

Karen's eyes were watery as Chandar helped her out of

her Dolce & Gabbana silk dress. She had on a light sky blue thong with a matching bra. She watched Chandar expectantly, looking for a sign of approval. Chandar admired her body and wondered how he let Shorty slip pass him for this long.

He removed his chain and medallion and laid it on the table. Next, he peeled off his wife beater, never letting his eyes leave Karen's beautiful body. Seductively, he stepped out of his shorts and Gucci underwear, and approached slowly. Grabbing her hand, he turned her around. Shorty was perfect! Chandar stepped closer and pressed his hardness against her ass. She felt his warm breath on her neck, and the smell of the wine and Bling-Bling cologne from John Tarik was in the air.

Chandar opened the clasps and removed her bra, before turning her around to face him.

Tears ran down Karen's face freely and Chandar gently tried to kiss each one of them. His dick was on her stomach, and she swiped a hand gently pass his balls and stroked the length of his manhood. Chandar put a hand under her chin and kissed her on the mouth. Karen's pussy was soaking wet! Chandar sucked on her tongue and reached around her to palm her ass.

"Take me," she whispered.

Chandar quickly put a finger to his lips! There was absolutely no need for words! His face was contorted into mock anger.

He took Karen's hand and led her down on the comforter, laying her on her back. He began kissing and sucking on her stomach, playing with her belly ring. She wanted him to head down south, but he was on his way up north. Her nipples were nice and hard! Chandar sucked them both and massaged her breast before biting on her nipples softly.

The sound of water falling into the fountain was exotic, and R. Kelly and Public Announcement blowing *Honey Love*

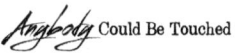 

was icing on the cake.

*'There's something in your eyes baby, that's telling me you want me baby. Tonight is your niiight.'*

Karen lifted up so Chandar could remove her thong, and then he was spreading her legs apart and cocking them back.

The flickering light of the candle could be seen through her eyes. Chandar entered her and she gasped. He couldn't believe how tight the pussy was! He took his time gliding his rock hard manhood further and further into her temple until it felt as if he couldn't go any further. Then he just started stroking, watching Karen as she was having difficulty breathing. He put one leg on his shoulder and kissed and sucked on it. As her pussy got wetter and adjusted to the dick, he was able to hammer it all the way, and Karen was fucking back.

*'Just like a lollipop, you're so sweet... And your body's like a lemon drop, sure taste good to me!'*

Chandar pulled out and helped Karen up. He bent her over the marble ledger of the fountain and began fucking her from the back. He had his hands on her hips and threw one of his legs on the ledger, and penetrated her like she was never penetrated before. A cool spray of water was hitting Karen's face. The friction on her clit allowed her to cum numerous times.

Afterward, Chandar laid down on his back and let Karen ride him. She bent down and put her tongue in his mouth, and he embraced her, holding her tightly until he exploded inside her. They stayed in each other's arms for what seemed like hours and then they got busy again. They made love until the sun came up, and then they went into the master bedroom and looked into each other's eyes until sleep overtook them.

Today Was a New Day.

# Chapter Thirteen

The grumble of thunder could be heard in the distance, just moments before the electrical blue lightning lit up the night sky.

A voice was telling Don Chi-Chi to stay in the house. It was the voice of India, his son's mother.

That voice, incorporated with a gut feeling, should've been enough to persuade the young gee to fall back for the night. It wasn't.

Don Chi-Chi was being pulled to his fate. He had enjoyed spending the afternoon with his son, Jermaine. Jermaine was only five years old, but Don Chi-Chi took him on a shopping spree and bought the little fella all that his little heart desired. The trunk and backseat of the GS was packed to capacity. Afterwards, they got haircuts at Cutty's on Hillside Avenue and Parsons Boulevard. They ate at McDonald's and Jermaine played on the slide and the small jungle gym, courtesy of the chain food giant.

Don Chi-Chi couldn't resist breezing through his cousin's block. Cue and his team were posted up in front of 20-20 Pacific Street when the GS400 pulled up to the curb. Don Chi-Chi jumped out playing the part of a true ghetto star to the tee. Everybody on the block showed the homie crazy love.

"Damn, nigga. What you went and did, robbed a bank,"

Cue asked with a smile. Don Chi-Chi was shining, and Cue wasn't a hater. He liked to see the next man shine, especially family.

"Nah yo! The big homie is home, and this is how he do," Don Chi-Chi said, pulling his cousin to the side before he continued. "I told him about you, and he wants to meet you, son. Word! We already got fourteen keys of coke and crazy spots he plotting on. Just between you and me, I think that nigga wants me and you to run the whole operation." Cue had his eyes wide open in shock at what his cousin had revealed.

"You serious," he asked.

"Like cancer," Don Chi-Chi responded.

"Well, you know if the numbers are right, I'm with whatever."

"Alright bet, I'm gonna pick you up around 8:30 tonight. I gotta go drop my son off and take care of a few things."

Don Chi-Chi gave his cousin dap and bounced. The few things he had to take care of was India. When he got back to the crib, his son was knocked out snoring. He carried him in the house and put him in bed. India was running around the house wearing a cut off t-shirt that exposed her belly and the bottom of her breast. The shorts she wore left little to the imagination! The print of her pussy automatically had Don Chi-Chi ready to do the damn thing, and when she turned around, her shorts were too short to contain her entire ass.

So, Don Chi-Chi handled his biz, and then caught a little nap. He woke up around 8:15, but something didn't feel right. His son was running around playing with his toys, and India was cooking something to eat. Don Chi-Chi felt like he was where he was supposed to be, with his family. He wanted to stay in the house and be a father and a good man to India. It didn't help when India pleaded for him to stay inside, and that was when he heard the faint sound of thunder in the distance. That was Don Chi-Chi's premonition!

He gave India $5,000 to put away for them, and $500 for herself, spending money. He gave his son a big hug and he was out the door. He never even got a chance to eat the meal that India prepared for him. He took for granted that it would be waiting for him in the microwave when he got home.

On his way to pick up his cousin in Brownsville, Don Chi-Chi noticed a white and blue police car behind him. The nine millimeter on his lap was quickly tossed under the driver's seat.

*'Damn, I knew I should've stayed in the house,'* he thought as he drove. As fate would have it, the cops found no reason to harass the young black male driving the luxurious vehicle through the ghetto.

Don Chi-Chi was able to pick up Cue and drive to Baisley Projects without incident.

Jerry Moore was posted up leaning against the fence of the basketball court on Foch Boulevard, between Guy R. Brewer Boulevard and Long Street. He had on jeans and a white-tee, crisp white on white Air Force Ones, and a platinum double-rivet floating canary cross that set him back forty grand. The big homie was blinging to a higher power! The diamonds in the cross were clear with a beautiful cut.

Jerry Moore's squad was on the scene, and despite the threat of rain, the atmosphere was charged. A-Blood was in the basketball court shooting around with some of the locals from Baisley; Sharod, BJ, Shane, Corey, and Gary. G-Bundles and Bugsy were posted up by the big homie's Benz, free styling. Tank was standing nearby, with his arms folded, watching niggaz play basketball, and Reggie Ransom was watching everything and everybody! The OG wouldn't let a potential threat within twenty feet of Jerry Moore.

When Lashawn and her girlfriends pulled up in her black Honda Accord, Reggie Ransom warned her, "Lashawn, listen to me. Next time, you might wanna park up the block. I didn't know who you were, and I can't be letting people get too close to main man. You understand?"

In other words, the psycho was on the verge of blowing holes in that Honda Accord if they hadn't made themselves known. Lashawn didn't catch that part of the message, but she didn't want to argue with the old head, so she agreed.

"My bad, I understand where you're coming from," she said, and then walked over to Jerry Moore.

"Your friend is burned the fuck out! He gonna try to dictate where I park my car like he own this block or something," she said before giving the big homie a hug.

"He's just watching my back, but what's up though?"

"Nothing, I was just driving pass and I saw you, so I stopped to see what's up with you."

"You tryin' to get your fuck on tonight?"

*This nigga don't know what to say out his mouth*, Lashawn thought, but she said, "It's whatever. I need some money! Me and my girlfriends are trying to get some weed, and I need gas."

Jerry Moore dug in his pocket and pulled out a brick of big faces. He passed Shorty a small stack.

"Go do what you do and hit me up later, about twelve," he instructed.

While Lashawn was leaving, Jerry Moore called Sharod from the other side of the fence. Sharod interrupted his game of basketball to see what the homie wanted.

"What's up, big homie?"

Jerry Moore pointed to a well-dressed female in her late twenties or early thirties. She was walking with a dirty crack head dude up the hill to building three.

"What's up with home girl right there?"

"Who, Sarah?"

"Yeah, that's her name? That's the second crack head looking nigga I saw Shorty with tonight. She getting high?"

"Nah, Sarah probably hustling. She do her thing every now and then, Shorty cool."

Jerry Moore made a mental note to do his homework on Shorty.

"Alright, good looking, son."

There was a Mister Softee ice cream truck on Foch Boulevard, down the hill from building three in Baisley, when Don Chi-Chi and his cousin pulled up.

Jerry Moore gave the man in the truck $500, and all the kids, and the grown-ups too, were eating ice cream for free.

Don Chi-Chi gave the big homie some dap and then made the introductions. Jerry Moore was genuinely happy to finally meet Cue. He needed thinkers on his team, and people who were good with numbers.

Don Chi-Chi went around the fence to the entrance of the basketball court, leaving his cousin alone with the big homie so they could feel each other out.

That's when Chandar's silver Porsche, followed by a black Escalade and a black Range Rover, pulled up in front of Don Chi-Chi's GS400.

The thunder roared and seconds later, lightning lit up the sky, implicating that the storm was getting closer.

Chandar, Wild Blood, O' Corleone, and Makavelli jumped out their whips, and it was almost like old times.

Reggie Ransom seldom smiled, but when he saw Chandar, his face lit up like the sun.

"Road dawg! It's good to see you," he hollered.

Deep down, anyone who knew Chandar and Jerry Moore, knew they complimented each other. Together, they were a supreme team! So no one who wanted good for them as individuals would want them to be beefing.

"OG, that ain't about nothing," Chandar responded, mocking the way Reggie Ransom spoke, but in a friendly way.

Chandar was carrying a red and black knapsack, similar to the one A-Blood gave Jerry Moore, and he dropped it at Jerry Moore's feet.

"You know I love you, right," Chandar asked, smiling at the homie.

Jerry Moore forgot about their little squabble and gave Chandar a hug!

"I love you back, big homie," Jerry Moore submitted.

"Give us a minute," Chandar said to Cue.

It seemed as if everybody in the projects was out, just

enjoying being in the presence of people who had enough money to make their own rules.

"I need to be back in Nevada tomorrow, but I'm gonna try to make it back in 2 weeks," Chandar said, and then continued. "I know you're not ready to take that trip with me as of yet, but I want you to think about it. I need you playa, bottom line! You got $250,000 in that bag. That should be enough to keep you out the street, right?"

Jerry Moore just smiled, and he answered evasively.

"I feel you!"

"It's about to pour down raining. But before I get ghost, I need you to promise me something."

"What's that homie," Jerry Moore asked.

Chandar placed a hand on his shoulder and looked him in the eye.

"Promise me we'll never let anybody, or anything come between us."

Jerry Moore nodded his head up and down.

"You got my word as a man, Chandelier. I'll never let anyone or anything break our bond," he said, using the nickname that he gave Chandar back in their school days.

That's when the first drops of rain began to fall. Everybody showed each other love, except for Don Chi-Chi and Chandar, and then they were jumping in their vehicles and peeling off.

It was pouring down rain, and Don Chi-Chi was on his

way to drop off his cousin Cue. He was going to have a night at home after all.

"Ayo, fire up that blunt in the ashtray," he instructed Cue.

"Shit, you don't have to tell me twice." Cue lit up the blunt and inhaled deeply.

"Jerry Moore seems like a good dude," he said as he exhaled smoke.

"That nigga might be one of the realest niggaz on the planet, ya heard," Don Chi-Chi said, and then continued. "I'm supposed to meet him at the studio tomorrow morning at eleven, you tryna roll?"

"No doubt! I wanna finish bustin' it up with him anyway. I'm trying to see how I could push one of them big boys, that white 600 is crazy!"

"In due time that's gonna be us, we just have to be patient, pass the blunt, nigga! Puff, puff, pass!"

"AH, AHH, AHHH," Cue said passing the blunt, and then continued. "Puff, puff, pass!"

Don Chi-Chi hit the blunt and looked out the rearview mirror. It was raining crazy hard, but he could've swore the same gray car was behind him for the longest.

"I think somebody is following us," he said, sitting the blunt in the ashtray.

Cue turned around in his seat and saw that there was a gray sports car behind them.

"Why you say that," Cue asked.

"Because that nigga been behind me damn near since we left the projects," Don Chi-Chi said putting on his blinkers to make a left turn.

Don Chi-Chi was already driving with his gun in his lap, and now Cue had his gun out and was jacking a round into the head.

Don Chi-Chi made the left turn and the gray car followed.

"Fool, that nigga is on my ass like tight draws," Chi-Chi yelled.

"Keep ya cool, fam! Bang another left."

"If this nigga follow me, we bangin' it out," Don Chi-Chi said, putting on his left blinker. He caught another left turn, but the grey car kept going straight.

"Let me find out you paranoid," Cue said laughing. Don Chi-Chi didn't respond, he just grabbed the blunt from out the ashtray and took three consecutive tokes to get it burning again.

That gray car was following him, he didn't care what Cue said. He looked at the blunt in his hand and hoped he wasn't being paranoid. Don Chi-Chi looked at the road and then over at his cousin. Cue was shaking his head, and then they both burst out laughing.

"Puff, puff, pass nigga," Don Chi-Chi said, passing Cue the blunt.

"Puff, puff, pass," Cue agreed.

Don Chi-Chi dropped Cue off and made his way home. It wasn't raining that hard anymore, and Chi-Chi was reflecting on his good fortune. He had a good girl, a wonderful son, a GS400 Lexus, and money in his pocket. This was the way life was supposed to be.

There was a parking space right in front of India's house.

Blueberry-Loc was trailing Don Chi-Chi for the longest

before the dude even knew he was being followed. B-Loc was in a silver G35 Infinity. When Don Chi-Chi figured out he had company, Blueberry-Loc made one turn with him, after that his mission was accomplished.

Nasty Nate and Jerome was in a black Navigator jeep following Don Chi-Chi from a safe distance. The rain helped to camouflage their mission.

Jerome Smith was the leader of the 121st Avenue Crips. He was originally from West Philly, but he was a suspect in a double homicide that forced him to migrate to the streets of Jamaica, Queens. He was a contract killer by profession, and Blueberry-Loc paid him between ten and twenty grand a job, depending on circumstances.

They came around the corner and was at a slow creep on India's block where Don Chi-Chi was parking his Lexus. Nasty Nate pulled up right beside the GS. Jerome was already leaning out the window gripping the chrome Four-Fifth.

Don Chi-Chi never saw it coming! He had his hand on the door handle ready to open the door when the bang of the iron pierced the silent night.

"Blop, blop, blop, blop, blop, blop, blop, blop, blop, blop, blop, blop, blop, blop!!!"

The sound of gunfire scared India out of her sleep! She looked to Don Chi-Chi's side of the bed and panicked when she saw that he wasn't there.

She heard the sound of tires screeching on the pavement, and she almost tripped over the coffee table in the living room trying to make it to the front window.

When she looked out the window, she covered her mouth

with both hands. Chi-Chi's new gold Lexus sat in front of her house, bullet riddled with the driver's side door slightly ajar. The interior light was on, and a body was slumped between the steering wheel and the driver's door.

"Chi-Chi," India screamed. "God, no! Please, don't let it be my baby! Chi-Cheeeee!"

Little Jermaine was crying. He was scared. Poor little fella... daddy went bye-bye!

# Chapter Fourteen

Flight 718 landed at Ontario International Airport at 1:40 PM; it was 4:40 PM New York time.

Jeff White had arranged for a limousine to pick up Chandar and Karen, and they were whisked away to Chandar's house in the hills of Moreno Valley, California.

Chandar was dead tired! He had spent the early morning hours with his mother, and sister, Pauline. He had taken them to breakfast. The night before, he hardly got any sleep. He was busy scraping up $300,000 in cash. 250 grand went to Jerry Moore, and 50 grand went to a dead friend's family.

Karen was just as exhausted. She did a ton of last minute packing, and she had to beg her sister, Regina, to manage the restaurant while she was gone. After finally getting Regina to agree, her next task was carefully instructing Regina on what to do. Karen's restaurant was her baby, and truthfully speaking, she didn't trust anyone when it came to her baby. If it had been anyone but Chandar, Karen would have never entertained the thought of doing something as impulsive as this.

They both were in first class nodding off, and Chandar was at peace when he would awake to find Karen sleeping on his shoulder.

Now they were in the limo, turning into the driveway of Chandar's four car garage.

Chandar's home was a large one story, made of red brick. There were four bedrooms, a living room, a dining room, an island kitchen, a home office, and a small exercise room. The backyard was huge, and was a part of a community that consisted of six homes. They all shared a small pond, a golf course, a batting range, and a picnic area.

Grandma Cynthia was in the doorway, and Jasmine came charging out the house to welcome her father home.

"Daddy," she screamed gleefully, as she ran into Chandar's arms. "I missed you, daddy!"

"I missed you too, Princess," Chandar said giving his daughter a smothering hug before he continued. "This is daddy's friend, Karen! Say hi!"

"Hi, daddy's friend, Karen!"

"And hello to you, Miss Jasmine," Karen said in her baby voice. Jasmine found that funny, and she was laughing.

"Daddy, where's my surprise?" Jasmine broke away and ran to the limo inspecting all the luggage crammed inside.

"Be patient, little mama. Let's focus on getting all this stuff inside."

Jasmine grabbed a small carry-on bag and hauled it in the house. The limo driver began unloading the rest of the luggage, most of the stuff belonged to Karen!

"Y'all kids need some help with all that stuff" Grandma Cynthia asked from the doorway.

"You just relax beautiful lady. I have someone special I want you to meet."

Jasmine was back for another bag. She tried to grab one that was almost bigger than her.

"Here, take this one." Chandar passed her a smaller bag.

When all the bags were inside, Chandar instructed the limo driver to come back and pick him up around 6 PM. He wanted to spend some quality time with Karen, and he wasn't in the mood to drive.

After introducing Karen to Grandma Cynthia, Chandar gave Karen a tour of the house before showing her to the guest room. Out of respect for Lisa's mother, and his daughter, that was the room that Karen would sleep in.

When Chandar showered and was settled in, he gave Jasmine her surprise. She was always talking about how some of her friends had cell phones, and she was persuasive in her argument of why she should have one.

Chandar didn't understand why an eight year old would need a cell phone, but he concluded that it wouldn't hurt, and he did see how it could be useful. He gave Jasmine a pink Razor Motorola; a cute little pink phone with two-way capabilities, access to the internet, a camera, and a walkie-talkie that allowed her to chirp her father for free anywhere in the country. Chandar also gave one to Grandma Cynthia.

At 6 PM, Karen was well rested. She took a long shower and came out smelling fresh and clean. She was wearing a sequence dress by Donna Karen that hugged her curvaceous body.

When the limousine arrived, Chandar took Karen to the Kara Spa at the Park Hyatt Hotel in Los Angles. The spas' concierge greeted them warmly.

"Madam, Sir, welcome to the Urban Kara Spa. My name is Kevin, and it is my wish to assist you in achieving your goals. We offer relaxation and invigoration for jet lag relief. We have nine treatment rooms, two of which are for couples only. Our heated tables-"

"Kevin, please. Breathe!" Chandar said, being kind yet assertive, and then continued. "Accommodate us with a treatment room for couples, and we'll have the 90 minute diamond miracle."

Kevin flashed a courteous smile. "But of course, Sir!"

They were escorted into a room that resembled a garden. The atmosphere was pleasant, and soft jazz played in the background. The treatment began with a foot soak and massage, and that was followed by a body scrub. Karen and Chandar enjoyed maximum eye contact but they barely spoke. They were being treated like a king and queen, and Karen thought she was in heaven.

A massage using oils with silk and pearl elements came next; and the treatment concluded with a facial that incorporated pure diamond dust.

Afterward, Chandar and Karen relaxed in lounge chairs, eating strawberries, and Karen sipped on the complimentary champagne.

"I am so relaxed right now," Karen said, closing her eyes, and then continued. "This is just what I needed."

Chandar was happy to be able to please. Once they were back in the limo, Karen mentioned that she was in the mood for Kentucky Fried Chicken. They went through the drive-thru of KFC before trekking across the desert to Las Vegas, Nevada; the gaming capital of the world.

Traveling down Howard Hughes Parkway, Karen was infatuated by all the lights and the energy of the city.

People of all nationalities, both genders, various ages, shapes and forms, were outside in droves, apparently having a good time.

"Look at all the people," Karen exclaimed.

"You should see it on fight night," Chandar said, sharing her excitement.

They drove past the MGM, and minutes later they were pulling in front of Sweet Dreams. Sweet Dreams was a medium size casino connected to the Philmore Hotel. There were over a hundred slot machines, and fifty tables advertising various card games to the patrons. Dice tables, and spinning wheel games encircled the card tables. Three cages were set up to exchange cash for chips, and vice versa. Staff members in burgundy aprons with pockets acted as mobile cash cages for small transactions. A huge island bar separated the slot machines from the tables catering to the heavy gamblers.

When Chandar and Karen walked through the automated glass doors, the floor manager was standing with his back to them. Chandar cleared his throat before addressing him.

"Excuse me, Mr. Bell?"

Infra-red turned around, and Karen's eyes got big as quarters! Infra-red was dressed immaculately, and his smile lit up the whole room.

"Oh my God! Inf," Karen screamed! She turned and punched Chandar in the arm, and then continued. "Chandar, that's not fair. Why you didn't tell me?"

Infra-red grabbed Karen's hand and gently planted a kiss on it. Next he gave Chandar a firm handshake.

"I would give both of you big hugs, but I'm working right now. Damn little sis', you look marvelous." Karen turned in a circle so Inf could admire her from head to toe.

"Thank you, brother!" Then she looked at Chandar. "He can't give me a hug?"

Chandar shook his head. "This is a place of business. It wouldn't look right for a floor manager to succumb to his emotions. He has to be on point, and disciplined."

*"Excuse me,"* Karen said with a smile. Chandar leaned over and kissed her on her lips. Inf was staring in disbelief!

"Yo! What the fuck was that," he yelled, losing his composure, looking at Chandar, then Karen, then back at Chandar.

Chandar's next words were almost enough to make Karen's heart skip a beat.

"I think I'm in love, playboy!"

For over a year, Chandar was the floor manager at Sweet Dreams. Prior to that, he had established Club International on the outskirts of Las Vegas for Anthony Orena.

Anthony Orena was a mob boss that Chandar met when the mobster was incarcerated with Jerry Moore at the Metropolitan Detention Center in Brooklyn. Jerry Moore was fighting drug conspiracy charges and Anthony Orena was serving a violation for leaving the country without permission while on parole. One day Chandar was visiting Jerry Moore and Mr. Orena was in the visiting room with his son; little Anthony. Jerry Moore made the introductions, and Mr. Orena invited Chandar to look him up if he was ever in Las Vegas.

Anthony Orena was so impressed with the clubs Chandar operated in New York, that when they finally met on the streets of Nevada he offered Chandar a job. Mr. Orena literally made an offer that Chandar couldn't refuse… 1.2 million a year, $250,000 up front.

The catch was that Mr. Orena wanted Chandar to open a casino in the territory of Sonny Womack, a well-connected wise-guy. That provided to be an amazing feat. In Nevada,

Chandar was out of his element, and the Italian Mafia was a colossal entity. Again, Jim Hightower's words rang true: 'Even a small dog can piss on a big building.'

Sonny Womack was a shrewd businessman and a cold blooded killer! He catered to a wealthy clientele that for one reason or another, couldn't, or refused to be seen in the public eye of Las Vegas. For this reason, Sonny set up shop along the outskirts of the city.

Sonny Womack's headquarters was a night club known as The Underground. The Underground was easily the most prosperous casino in the outer limits of Vegas. Still, Sonny had a motto: "Any establishment operating on my side of town, has to pay!"

Chandar visited The Underground several times to see what he could learn about his opponent. He found out that Sonny Womack was an old man in his late 60's... Sonny frequented his club regularly... And there were metal detectives at the door, and a top of the line security staff situated strategically throughout the club.

On Chandar's third visit, he learned that The Underground was far from impenetrable. The bathroom had a window with bars on it that opened to an alley that ran along the side of the club.

Chandar had an idea! He sent Infra-red back to New York to find an old friend, a junkie name Kenny that had less than six months left to live.

Kenny had full blown AIDS, and his T-Cell count was so low, that it was amazing he wasn't in the hospital. Instead, he was busy searching for places to stick the next heroin filled needle.

Kenny was pitiful, and he no longer even had a desire to live. His only regret was that he had nothing to leave his sister to help her with her kids. Kenny's mother and father both died from AIDS. So whenever death came to claim his soul, his sister would be alone.

Infra-red found Kenny in East New York, trying to scrape up enough money to get a fix. He gave Kenny money to get off 'E' and promised him a pot of gold at the end of the rainbow.

Infra-red arrived in Nevada with Kenny in tow, looking sickly, yet fresh and clean.

Chandar expressed his condolences to Kenny, for his plight was truly a sad one. Then he inquired about Kenny's sister, Marie.

The only reason Kenny allowed Infra-red to lure him to the airport and on a plane was because of the promise of an endless supply of dope. Now his conversation with Chandar made him feel shameful as he thought of his little sister, Marie. Kenny began to cry!

"I fucked up Chandar! She has nothing, and I'm nothing but a dope fiend. Look at me, man! I just travelled coast to coast for a fix. What am I gonna do?"

"Do you love Marie," Chandar asked.

"Of course I do, man! She's all I got in this world. And when I'm gone, she'll have no one," Kenny cried.

Chandar hugged Kenny and pulled him close.

"I want to help you, Kenny... But I need you to help me, help you."

"I'll do anything Chandar, anything!"

So Chandar laid out the plan.

The Underground was crowded when Kenny entered the club, looking dapper in a green silk suit with green Gucci alligator slip-ons. He cleared the metal detectors and walked past the table where Sonny Womack was telling a war story to an audience of beautiful women.

Kenny made his way to the bar for a drink, a double shot of Vodka, and then he went straight to the bathroom. He made sure all the stalls were empty before he opened the window that led to the alley, where Infra-red passed him a Glock 40 fully loaded.

Kenny had already made up his mind. He would do what he had to do to make sure his sister and his nieces and nephews would be taken care of after he died. He checked the clip of the Glock 40 and jacked a bullet in the chamber before concealing the gun on his waist. He took a deep breath and then walked out into the club to handle his business.

Sonny was still at the table laughing and enjoying life, oblivious to the impending danger. Kenny observed two of Sonny's personal security trying to be inconspicuous. The element of surprise was on his side. He walked right up to the table where Sonny was at and pulled out the Glock, aiming it at Sonny.

"You killed Bub," Kenny shouted. He noticed the look of shock on Sonny Womack's face, and then there was fear. He squeezed the trigger repeatedly, and the club went into pandemonium.

Sonny Womack dropped face first into the table! Kenny spun to the security man on the left and lifted him off his feet. He thought if he could only get the man to his right, there was a possibility he could make it out of there alive and maybe get one more fix.

It was too late! The security man had drawn his 9mm and the barrel was raised. Kenny tried to spin around, blasting as he turned, but the security man was faster! He put two shells in

Kenny's dome, and then as an afterthought, he blessed him with one more. Kenny hit the floor, but his mission was accomplished. Sonny Womack was dead… and Marie, and the kids, would be taken care of.

After that incident, establishing Club International was a piece of cake. Chandar was once again victorious.

Chandar went to one of the cages and got $1,000 worth of chips so Karen could enjoy herself at the casino. When they exhausted themselves, they retired to Chandar's condo at 2900 S. Highland.

Chandar was in love, but so was Karen, and this was a lifestyle that she could easily get used to.

# Chapter Fifteen

The kid was on a path of self-destruction from the beginning! It was no wonder that his teachers thought he wouldn't amount to nothing. Don Chi-Chi's cousin, Cue, held a summer job once, for the Summer Youth Program, and that lasted for about 3 weeks. He was a counselor at Day Camp for Kids between the ages of 8 and 12, and there were numerous complaints filed that Cue was beating on the kids. As if that wasn't enough, the last straw was when he got caught masturbating off of one of the female supervisors.

"She knew what I was doing. She liked it," was his sick way of reasoning.

Then there was a job that he held at McDonald's. That may have lasted for a whole month and a half! He resigned from Mickey Dee's because, "That 9 to 5 shit just ain't me!"

The truth was, Cue was a night person. And let's face it, he felt as if he was destined to live the street life... It was in his blood! Cue's father was a hustler, and his mother, unfortunately, fell victim to the harsh reality of drug addiction.

As ironic as it may seem, this was a blessing as a well as a curse as far as Cue was concerned. He loved his mother dearly, and if the opportunity presented itself, he would quickly sacrifice his own life for hers. Still, he hated that his mother became what society labeled being a crack head. He hated the humiliation that he faced, the people knowing and talking behind his back, the shame he sometimes felt when he saw her on the streets... To Cue, this was a curse. He prayed to God to help his mother. He asked God to protect her and to free her from her addiction. Then there were times that he questioned God's existence. *'If there is a God, why would He let this happen? Why won't He answer my prayers?'*

As Cue got older, he learned to accept and love his mother for who she was. He also began to see the blessing!

It was his mother who introduced him to the game! She taught him how to cook cocaine into crack, she taught him how to flip his money, and she schooled him on how to establish and keep clientele. It was also his mother that introduced him to the Jamaicans that had a stronghold on 20-20 Pacific Street

Cue's mother often cooked up for the dreads, and they had so much love for her that they allowed her son to put work on their block. This was a come up for Cue, because 20-20 Pacific Street was a goldmine in crack sales. Cue was hugging the block from sunup to sundown, and each day his stash and his supply escalated. As the Jamaicans grew fond of having Cue around and Cue got comfortable being in their presence, he began to establish his own team on the block. He brought in Patches, and Blind, and as time went on, he brought in Don Chi-Chi.

Cue decided he would keep the spot on Pacific Street poppin' no matter what. He had invested too much time and energy. Whatever Jerry Moore required of him, he would hold that down too... It was time to take his hustle to the next level.

Cue looked at his watch... It was going on 1:00 in the afternoon! Don Chi-Chi was supposed to pick him up at eleven. Cue pulled out his cell phone and dialed India's number for the fifth time, but it was still busy. He then placed a call to Chi-Chi's cell phone, and he was sent to voicemail. Cue had Jerry Moore's cell phone number, but he didn't want the big homie to think he was sack riding, so he fell back.

He waited for a whole hour to pass before trying India's number again. This time the call went through… It was 2 PM.

"Hello?!?"

"India, what's up? It's Cue! Where ya husband at?" India started crying hysterically, and she was trying to speak, but she was incoherent. "India calm down. I can't understand you! What happened?"

"He was in the car… My son is going to grow up without a father," India sobbed.

"What are you talking about? Where's my cousin???"

"He's dead, Cue! They killed him!"

"What???"

"He's dead!"

Cue was silent on the line as he digested what he just heard. This couldn't be happening! Shit was just starting to get good.

"CUE," India screamed into the phone.

"Yo!"

"What are you doing???"

"I'm tryin' to make sense out of what you just told me. I mean, damn… I was just with him yesterday."

"Where are you???"

"I'm on the block," Cue said, and then continued. "But I'm on my way over."

"Please, hurry!"

When Cue ended the call, he was already walking to

his car. He needed to be there for India and Jermaine! He also needed to inform Jerry Moore that there was a casualty of war. He opened his cell phone and dialed the number.

Jerry Moore was in studio 'B' at Loud Mouth Records. Del Gibson was a no show in the building, something came up at the last minute so he couldn't make it. Never the less, he left instructions with Simoya to make sure the big homie had access to anything he needed. KC, one of the engineers, was at his disposal. Also, Maxwell Smart was hanging around like an obedient puppy, so Jerry Moore had him cook up some hot tunes.

Also in studio 'b' was G-Bundles, AKA Gino, and his partner in rhyme, Bugsy. They were ready to lay some vocals for their mixtape. Both of them were high as shit, and they were playing with flows and burping on the microphones while Maxwell Smart was looking for the perfect beats to jack, and KC ensured that the sounds were parallel.

When Maxwell Smart was ready with the perfect track to set it off with, he instructed G-Bundles and Bugsy to spit some ad-lib. They bullshitted for about 10 minutes shouting out themselves and Jerry Moore, and spitting bars and harmonizing, until Maxwell Smart heard what he wanted to hear.

"Okay, listen…Give the brief introduction and the shout out to the big homie, then I want y'all to go straight into the 'Death to all Those' routine that you were doing. Repeat the chorus twice without the music, and I got something nice for you when y'all finish. Let's do it on a three count… O'kay, one… Two… one, two, Three!"

G-Bundles and Bugsy had their headphones on and they were standing in front of 2 mics!

"I don't need no intro, y'all know who the fuck I be…G-Bundles!"

"Gangsta for real- Bugsy in this bitch!"

"We just wanna welcome the big homie home in style-

"Jerry Moore!"

"Gansta stand up! This is for my niggaz… if ya gun bust / death to all those who go against us! / this is for my niggaz, if ya gun bust / death to all those who go against us!"

Maxwell Smart let the beat drop! It was the instrumental to Jay-Z's *Can't Knock the Hustle.*

"Yes! Here we go!"

"I'm not a king, but I had a dream I changed my ways / my flow sick like a fiend that ain't been high for days / you wanna know what I mean, I like to cock AK's / you don't know what I mean, then ya block get blazed / when I blow, I like it green and purple- cop that Haze / when it's slow on the scene, I flood the block with tray's / cut dope with Morphine, make 'em scratch and nod / annihilate ya whole squad, then I'm snatching ya broad."

"Don't make me spaz on these niggaz / niggaz don't get the picture / pictures are being taken / niggaz studying faces / faces disappear- it's hell or heaven / I go hard when it's time like 9-11 / eleven to seven, favorite gun: Mac 11 / throw up eleven hundreds like I'm going to heaven / at 12 o' clock, look at Ock, pushing the drop / candy apple red, it's the Bloods, ready to pop!"

"Pop, poppin' Cristal / shady individu-al wanna be a gener-al / peep my style, I'm wild! / mother fuckers chill with that bullshit / niggaz on some other shit / these niggaz gonna feel it / full clip up in my AK / from south side to BK / I'll have these faggot niggaz yelling: May day! May day! / mother fuckers think I'm craz-zey / and you can't blame it on the way my momma raised me / down and dirty, some crab niggaz tried to herb me / your little guns don't disturb me, ya heard me / it's ludicrous… preposterous / I'm thinking muderistic thoughts, smoking cannabis / I can handle this, niggaz that we all heard of / are screaming for the sex, money, murder! / You don't know? / It's all about the cash flow / that's what I said- Peace Blood, come on, paint da town red! / You're my niggaz… If ya gun bust / death to all those who go against us!"

"You're my mutha fuckin' niggaz, if ya gun bust / death to all those who go against us!"

Jerry Moore was posted up watching how everybody was playing their part. The big homie was satisfied! Gino and Bugsy were spitting that fire! He listened as they laced two more tracks; the B.I.G. *Who Shot ya* beat, and Jadakiss' *Knock ya self Out*, and then he stepped out the studio to get some air. He wondered what the hell happened to Don Chi-Chi, the homie was supposed to come through at eleven.

Jerry Moore looked at his watch… It was 2 PM.

'I cop this nigga a Lex, now he wanna act up!' the big homie thought. That's when his phone rang! He looked at the caller ID but didn't recognize the number, he answered it anyway.

"Yo! What's up?"

"Big homie?"

"Yeah, who this?"

"It's Cue… I got some bad news."

# Chapter Sixteen

The CEO of Loud Mouth Records was a very important man! Consequently, he was always busy. There was always an important meeting to attend, a lunch date, a phone call to be made, and even the things that he considered trivial demanded his attention.

However, Del Gibson made his own rules! He would be courteous to his business associates, and he would accommodate them when he was able, but when he needed a moment to breathe, or some quality time with loved ones... he made time! The company could be in the midst of a crisis, it didn't matter, when Doctor Hyde decided he needed some down time he would take it.

That was the case on May 1st, when Del was supposed to meet Jerry Moore at the studio. It was no disrespect to Jerry Moore, but May 1st was Deja's birthday. Deja was Del's 9 year old daughter. At first, Del was going to pick Deja up around 4 PM and pamper her for the rest of the evening; but when he woke up that morning, he decided he wanted to spend the entire day with his baby girl. So that's exactly what he did!

Bright and early, he took Deja to the beauty parlor to get her hair done, and then they shopped for a birthday outfit. Back at the house, they showered and got dressed, and by the time they finished a light breakfast, a helicopter was landing on the front lawn.

"Look Daddy, a helicopter," Deja squealed with delight.

"Are you ready to go,"" Del asked, smiling at his daughter.

"In the helicopter?" Deja asked.

"Yep!"

"No Daddy, I'm scared!"

"Don't be! Daddy's not going to let anything happen to you."

That was enough for Deja to feel safe. They ducked low under the spinning propellers and boarded the helicopter, and the pilot whisked them away.

Twenty minutes later, they were landing at the heliport atop the AT&T building in Manhattan. Del Gibson enjoyed the short trip from his home in Providence, Rhode Island, but Deja enjoyed it more. Normally it took some getting used to the quick jerks, swoops, and swerves of a helicopter ride, but Deja was a natural. She felt a little light-footed and dizzy afterwards, but it was worth it.

As they departed the AT&T building, Sabrina was awaiting patiently for them with the May Bach double parked on the street. Del helped his daughter into the backseat and then jumped in behind her. Sabrina, with prearranged instructions, drove them straight to the Beacon Theater.

They went to see a play called King of the Jungle, directed by a new up and coming black director name Shannon Williams. It was an entertaining, family oriented play about Lions and their struggle against hyenas and other beast of the jungle. Del almost fell asleep, but he fought the urge. And he managed to appear to be just as excited about the lions as Deja was. He really wanted her to enjoy her day!

Nevertheless, the big dawg was relieved when the show was finally over. He looked at his cell phone and he had seventeen messages! They would have to wait, today was all about Deja.

They went to eat at Tad's Steak Pub, and Del was proud of Deja's manners. She was behaving like a mature young lady. He had done a good job as a father! His children, Shaquan, Deja, Chivous, and Khalif would never want for anything! Del promised himself that he would be there for them in every way possible. Since his own father didn't seem to care for him, his brother, Anthony, and his sister, Tranee ... he promised he'd never do that to his seeds.

After they ate the main course meal, the manager of the restaurant brought a cake to the table with nine candles on it. Deja made a wish, and blew the candles out, and that's when Del saw her! A blast from the past, and she was staring in his direction! Del knew that face from anywhere, he would be able to pick her out of a crowd of a thousand people, and now she was only three tables away! She stood and wiped her hands on a napkin before making her way to their table. Del stood to greet her.

"Ericka!"

The day after Don Chi-Chi was killed, Del Gibson and his daughter weren't the only ones to attend the theater. Blueberry-Loc and his Uncle Ray went to see a play on Broadway, also. Ray wanted a closer relationship with his nephew, he wanted to try to prevent him from making some of the same mistakes he once made.

As usual, Ray was dressed immaculately in a tailor made silk suit from Italy, and Blueberry-Loc was dressed to impress in a Ralph Lauren Black Label suit. They had the appearance of wealth, and everywhere they would go people would steal glances at them while others would openly stare.

During an intermission, Ray went and ordered a shot of Jack Daniels. Being warmed by the drink, he decided now was a good time to try to get through to his nephew.

"Say, Kevin. Let me ask you a question... Where do you see yourself five years from now?"

The question caught Blueberry-Loc off guard. He never really gave it any thought, he didn't even know if he would be alive in five years.

"I'm just taking it one day at a time, Uncle Ray. Tomorrow is promised to no one."

"All that's well and true, nephew, but all successful people have goals! You have to get out there and make something happen or this world will chew you up and spit you out! You can't wallow in misery, and you can't wait for someone else to do something for you, do you understand? Of course you do, you're a bright kid! You can be CEO of your own company, you can earn a Doctorate Degree ... you can do *anything* if you put your mind to it. Now, tell me... What are you interested in? The stock market? The garment industry? Do you like computers and shit, everything is on the Internet these days and people are getting rich off of it. What do you want to do, Kevin?"

Blueberry-Loc pondered the question. He knew that his uncle meant well, but he truly didn't know what he wanted out of life besides revenge. He was like a blind man. He couldn't see the big picture of opportunity that his Uncle Ray was painting for him. He was too busy being driven by hate, and it was sad. He was wasting energy that he could've benefitted from by doing something positive. Blueberry-Loc was on a path of self-destruction!

"I don't know," was his simple response.

128

Ray looked at the boy like he was crazy! He told the man at the concession stand to pour him another shot of Jack Daniels.

"You don't know," Ray asked in amazement. He threw back the shot of Jack Daniels and paid the man before continuing. "Well, I strongly suggest you start thinking about it! You're not doing anything with your life, not that me and your mother are aware of. Don't be like the animals, Kevin. All they do is eat and sleep. I love you too much to stand by and watch you waste your life. Do something with yourself, nephew, go out there and be somebody!"

"Give me to September 1st... 120 days! Actually 122 days! Today is May 1st, there's 31 days in May, 31 days in July... by September 1st, I'll be enrolled in school or some kind of training program, or I'll be prepared to start my own business. I got you Uncle Ray... I promise you, I'm not gonna let you down."

"Wow! I thought that was you," Ericka said, giving Del a big hug.

"Ericka, this is my daughter, Deja! It's her birthday. Deja meet Ericka, she lives in Rhode Island, too. We use to work together."

"Hi," Deja said cheerfully.

"Happy birthday! How old are you," Ericka asked with a genuine smile.

"Nine!"

"Wow! This must be exciting for you, celebrating your ninth birthday. I remember my ninth birthday, I was thrilled!"

"Ericka, please, join us," Del invited, his mind was flooded with old memories.

Back in the day, Del had a job at the Salvation Army on Broad Street in Providence, Rhode Island. He was a counselor at the day camp, and so was Ericka. At the time, Ericka White was also studying at Providence Community College to become a lawyer.

Baby girl was a dime, and she was headstrong, so Del Gibson was impressed with her from day one, because he couldn't stand a punk ass bitch.

However, around Del, Ericka would never put her guard down. She knew Del had a crush on her, but she didn't trust him, and she rejected all of his passes, in a smooth way. And that, of course, kept him after her. Del loved a challenge.

He was eventually able to pierce her armor slightly, but she would always comment on his street ways, and his bad attitude. She even called him immature because he had a mouth full of gold teeth. Without saying it directly, she made it clear that he wasn't on her level.

Then one day, Del found out that she really did like him and was definitely interested. He was already use to her rejections and figured that he would never be intimate with her, when out of the blue, unexpectedly, she put the ball in his clutches and dropped a kiss on him! Mr. Del Gibson, all-American athlete, fumbled the ball… he froze like a deer caught in headlights!

"I really shouldn't," Ericka was saying, snapping him out of his reverie. "I'm here with my friend and her fiancé. You remember Ronnie, don't you?"

"Of course I do. That's Ronnie over there? Ronnie," Del said aloud, causing people to turn around.

Ronnie whispered something to her fiancé, and then made her way to the table. It was almost like a high school reunion.

"Del, you look good! This is your daughter? She's

adorable," Ronnie screamed.

They did some quick catching up, and then Del took the lead. "Listen Ronnie… go back over there with your fiancé, Ericka was probably in the way anyhow. I'll make sure she gets home safe, and I'll get your number from her so we can finish catching up."

"You are still crazy! Are you okay with that, Ericka?"

Ericka looked at Del.

"She's okay! Right, Deja?"

Deja nodded her head up and down, so Ericka went and got her purse and belongings and joined Del and his daughter.

Del learned that Ericka passed the bar examination and she was now a practicing lawyer. Ericka learned that Del was a chief executive officer of his own record label. Del learned that Ericka was single with no kids. Ericka learned that Del had four kids but wasn't married or involved with anyone. Del learned that Ericka was still headstrong. Ericka learned that Del still harbored feelings for her.

They enjoyed their meals, and afterwards, Ericka enjoyed the ride with them in the MayBach. She was impressed, but what really blew her mind was the helicopter atop the AT&T building waiting to whisk them back to Rhode Island.

Del Gibson was doing big things, and this was definitely a life that Ericka could easily get used to. When the helicopter landed on Del's front lawn, Deja was fast asleep!

"I think it's safe to say that she enjoyed her birthday." Del said proudly.

# Chapter Seventeen

Two weeks had passed since Big Time had copped his first big eighth. Since then, he replenished his stash three times! The last time he went uptown, he went with 5 grand, and his connect, Cheecho, blessed him with 10 ounces.

Shit was looking real good for the home team! Most of the little dudes on The Bully submitted and opted to work for Big Time. He was able to give them work on consignment, and then they would compete for the retail sales.

Kool-Aid was still bagging his half up in nickels, and it was hard for the other little dudes to compete with him because Kool-Aid had more coke then they did, so he would make his bottles fatter than theirs.

Still, everybody on The Bully was eating, and they were content. Thanks to Big Time and Kool-Aid, their hustle was seeing some progress.

"Feel me on this, Kool-Aid," Big Time said. They were sitting at the counter in Feaster's waiting for Ms. Debbie to make them some of her famous cheeseburgers. "On this next flip, I'm trying to cop me a hooptie, so we gotta bring everything back. We still got about a gee to play with but I need us to go see Cheecho with at least ten this time. What you think about that?"

Kool-Aid was a good dude, and he appreciated everything that Big Time had done for him; as a result, he had his boy's

back!

"I think that's a good idea, because we spend entirely too much money on cabs. I bagged up 7,500 off my half this time, I got 7 for you."

Big Time looked at his partner thoughtfully, and nodded his head.

"I told you we got about a gee to play with. Just give me 6,500 and we're straight. We gotta go cop a half a bird, and more than likely, Cheecho will bless us with something extra."

"What kinda whip you tryin' to get?"

"I got my eye on this black Nissan Altima. They only want 6 grand for it, but I'm trying to cop it for 5."

Ms. Debbie placed two of her famous cheeseburgers on the counter in front of them. Big Time started punishing his burger, but Kool-Aid still had something on his mind. His next words gave Big Time the creeps, and it was almost enough to make him lose his appetite. He spoke in a hushed tone...

"Damn, son. I wonder what happened to Chuck."

Mr. Kopell needed an extra week to deliver the K500 to Jerry Moore. The customized stretch S-Class wasn't due on the market for another year, so Mr. Kopell was fighting to secure clearance. Meanwhile, Jerry Moore gave Del Gibson 85 grand to make arrangements so he could keep the white S600. The big homie wanted to present the 600 to Cue as a gift, on the strength of Don Chi-Chi. Jerry Moore had gone to the homie's funeral, and afterwards, he went back to India's house and participated in the family gathering. There was plenty of food, there was laughing and crying, and Jerry Moore got to meet and spend time with Don Chi-Chi's son, Jermaine.

The big homie was hurt by the whole ordeal. He couldn't believe that Chandar would take things to this extreme. Never the less, he kept his thoughts concerning Chandar to himself, and acted as if Don Chi-Chi's killer was unknown to him. Jerry Moore sat down with Cue and India, and assured India that her and her son would be well taken care of. India was to see Cue if she needed anything!

After the insurance company paid to repair the GS400, Jerry Moore took India back to the car lot that they purchased the GS from, and they traded it in for a 5 series BMW Wagon for India. It was the least that Jerry Moore could do.

On the illegal side, Jerry Moore was still sitting on the 14 keys of coke that they repossessed from Chuck. In addition to that, A-Blood had taken 200 grand from the quarter million that Chandar gave Jerry Moore, and two days later he returned with twenty bricks of pure cocaine, and a piece of advice...

"Let's not make this a habit."

Now that the big homie was sitting on 34 kilograms of raw, uncut, cocaine ... It was time to make a move!

The squad was posted up in the basketball court in front of building 3 in Baisley. Jerry Moore was greatly troubled by the fact that Chandar had betrayed him, but in public he displayed the poker face. A-Blood had been adamant about the fact that Chandar had decided to give Don Chi-Chi a pass.

*'That fool rocked us to sleep,'* Jerry Moore thought.

He looked at the people surrounding him. Reggie Ransom was a one man army! He was skilled in the art of war, and a basic necessity to the team. Gino and Bugsy was their meal ticket on the legal side, he needed to keep them out of trouble. Cue was a thinker, he had the potential to run an entire operation... Plus he was Don Chi-Chi's cousin, so the big homie was adamant on letting him do him. And then there was Tank...

Tank was a genius. He would be responsible for making the dirty money clean.

"Ayo, listen…" Jerry Moore began, looking into the eyes of his people. "We're about to turn this shit up! Reggie Ransom, I need you to put together a team of gunslingers… If they can't be trusted, I don't wanna fuck with them! When the time come I need to know they're gonna bang that iron! Cue, you're the quarterback! Reggie Ransom and his team are gonna be your defensive line. You got yourself a dream team, take advantage of it! Supthin Boulevard is a gold mine! I want y'all to take from 114th Road, all the way to 121st Avenue. I want the whole Boulevard on lock! Reggie, take the car and jet to 112th and Guy R. Brewer real quick. I wanna see the twins, Teddy and Eddie. Bring them niggaz here!"

Jerry Moore tossed the keys to the Benz to Reggie Ransom, and Reggie went to follow out orders. The big homie continued, "Gino, we're depending on you and Bugsy to finish that mixtape! The quicker y'all finish and take that music thing to another level, the quicker we can get out these streets. Tank, you start putting together a plan to clean this money up… Dammit man, hold up for a minute!"

Jerry Moore lost his chain of thought… He was distracted by Sarah walking up the hill with a crack head. Shorty had some big ass titties! The big homie waited until she was in the building before he followed her. When he got inside the building, Sarah and the crack head just got on the elevator and the door was closing. Just before the elevator door completely shut Jerry Moore pushed the button and it opened back up. As the big homie entered the elevator, Sarah's eyes dropped to the platinum cross and chain hanging from his neck.

"That cross is real nice, how much you paid for it," she asked as the elevator door closed.

135

"They wanted 50 for it, but I only paid 45," Jerry Moore said nonchalantly as the elevator ascended to the 8th floor.

"45 what? Hundred," she asked boldly. Jerry Moore was used to it. Chicks in the projects was crazy nosey! He just shook his head.

""Thousand," Sarah continued to pry.

The big homie nodded in the affirmative.

"I could've bought me a car with that money," Sarah exclaimed as the elevator door opened. The crack head looked at the big homie's jewels like he wanted to snatch and run, but he must've seen something in Jerry Moore's eyes that told him he'd better keep it the fuck moving.

Sarah and the crack head got off the elevator and made a left. They went into one of the apartments by the incinerator. Jerry Moore stood in the hallway and waited for them to come back out.

In less than 5 minutes he heard someone unlock a door, and then Sarah and the crack head were walking to the elevator pushing the button.

"Sarah, you hear me? Let me speak to you for a minute," Jerry Moore stated smoothly.

"How you know my name?"

"It's my job to be aware of my surroundings," the big homie responded.

The crack head was holding the elevator door, waiting for Sarah.

"You can let the elevator go, she'll catch up with you later," Jerry Moore said, one eye up and one eye down. The crack head was trying to go get high anyway… He broke out like a rash.

"What you want to talk to me about," Sarah asked.

"You're a beautiful young lady! You dress nice, I see you like the finer things... I wanna make you a business proposition."

Sarah smiled. "I'm listening."

"Every time I see you, you're surrounded by crack heads... And you don't look like the type that smoke, so I'm assuming you're getting your hustle on. How much coke you working with?"

"I'm not gonna lie, I do hustle, but it's never nothing big. I buy an ounce or two at a time, and I got my personal clientele. It's just enough to feed my daughter and buy some things I like."

"How many other people that you know of is out here hustling?"

Sarah looked up at the ceiling and crunched up her face as she thought.

"A lot of people.... Maybe six or seven guys be out here on a regular basis."

"Okay, listen, this is what I'm prepared to do for you. I'm gonna ban everyone from hustling in these projects! Everybody except you! I already spoke to Big Ive, he's cool with whatever I do. You don't have to worry, I got the muscle to do this shit, but I'm gonna need you to hold it down... 24-7! If somebody sells a crack head a hit out of their personal pipe, it's gonna be your crack they're smoking. Anybody that wanna hustle in Baisley, they're gonna hustle for you! My team will help you find workers, and they'll provide security, but we'll be depending on you to ensure that the operation is running smooth. If you're serious about buying you a car, I can have two kilos delivered to you tonight, and we can start this shit up as early as tomorrow... It's up to you."

Sarah couldn't believe her good fortune! She was about

to get rich, and this thug ass nigga was looking good. So, she thought, if she played her hands right, she might even get some dick.

"I'm gonna need money for capsules!"

"You're not gonna use capsules, you're gonna use bags… all of that will be provided."

When the big homie got back outside, Teddy and Eddie were inside the basketball court. Reggie Ransom had them hemmed up like they were in public school and he was the bully!

When the big homie approached them, they avoided eye contact. These little niggaz was scared to death! Jerry Moore got straight to business.

"Y'all fools know who I am," he asked.

They both nodded their heads, and Teddy spoke. "Yeah, we know who you are, big homie!"

"Well 112th and Guy R. Brewer is mine, and I don't wanna talk about this no more! Now, I'm only gonna ask y'all once, is there a problem with what I just said?"

They both shook their head, and Teddy spoke: "Nah, that ain't no problem, big homie!"

Jerry Moore hated cowards, but he didn't think these little niggaz were cowards. They just knew who to fuck with and who not to fuck with.

"Y'all niggaz trying to get some money?"

They both nodded their heads, and Teddy spoke. "Yeah, we're with whatever, big homie!"

"Y'all niggaz come see me tonight about 8, I got a brick

apiece for y'all. I'm sending some of my people down there too. Don't fuck that money up! And when y'all see that nigga Gee who y'all was buying your weight from, let that nigga know what time it is and tell him to come see me."

Jerry Moore sent the twins on their way! The operation in Baisley was ready to go in motion, and now 112th and Guy R. Brewer was also ready. Now all the big homie had to do was orchestrate the takeover of The Bully!

He called Cue over and spoke to him briefly before he was interrupted by a phone call.

Cue stepped to the side and pulled out a small notepad and pen. He began playing with numbers.

When Jerry Moore got off the phone, Cue told him what he came up with.

"I figured using the 58-58 bags, we'll get up to 1300 an ounce. Off the 30 ounces, we'll bag up 39,000."

"Fuck is you talking about, homie?"

"You said you was gonna give me thirty O's, I was just doing the math."

Jerry looked at Cue with a smirk! "Homie, I didn't say I can hit you with thirty O's. What I said was I could supply you with thirty of those!"

Cue had a huge smile on his face as he pulled back out his pen and pad… It was time to add some zeros!

# Chapter Eighteen

Chandar was in love with the west coast! He would represent Brooklyn until the day he died, but he was slowly but surely switching sides. He didn't even like the Knicks anymore! He had season tickets to the Lakers games, and he occupied his seats every time he got a chance.

Chandar was comfortable on the west coast and the weather was amazing. His home was something straight out of Dupont Registry, and his job was in Las Vegas, that alone was enough to guarantee excitement.

In Chandar's twenty-five years on the planet, he spent most of his life struggling. Now he was finally getting a chance to live. It had been over a week since Karen flew into California with him, and he made sure she had a ball! They went everywhere! They took Jasmine with them to Universal Studios, Disneyland, Castle Park, and the Chinese Museum. When they were alone, they walked down Hollywood Boulevard together and took pictures of the stars on the ground that were dedicated to the rich and famous.

"If you keep doing the things you're doing, one day they're gonna have your name in one of these stars," Karen teased.

Chandar grabbed her in a bear hug and smothered her with kisses. He really felt comfortable around Karen! With her, he was able to put his guard down.

One day, they were driving through Beverly Hills with the top down on the SL600, and Chandar's song came on; *Let's Stay Together* by Al Green. Chandar started singing aloud with the song, tearing that joint up, but he felt no shame.

**"I I I I... I'm so in love with you... Whatever you want to do... It's alright with meeeeeee!"**

Karen had never seen this side of Chandar before! It was so innocent and childlike, her heart was softened.

**"Let me, be the one, you neeed..."**

Chandar was smiling, but he was feeling himself!

He and Karen did some shopping on Melrose Place. There were people everywhere, but Karen and Chandar were in their own little world! With Chandar, Karen felt complete. It was like they were soul-mates, and Chandar hadn't felt that way with anyone since Lisa.

One night, they were making love on the rug in front of the fireplace. Afterwards, they fell asleep in each other's arms. Chandar woke up in the middle of the night and Karen was already up scribbling in a notebook.

"What you doing, fat head," he asked in a sleepy voice.

"I'm writing you a letter," she responded.

"Let me see."

"Wait a minute."

Karen finished writing what she was writing and then passed the notebook to Chandar. As he began to read, she cuddled up on the rug watching him.

*Dear Chandar,*

*Words alone can't express how I'm feeling right now. This spur of the moment vacation is phenomenal! I would never have guessed, in a million years, that you and I would connect on this level. When you touch me, I feel chills! The look in your eyes when you desire me, makes me wet! Boo, I hate to sound insecure, but I never want this to be over. I'm talking about you and me! If there's anything you know about me, Chandar, it's that I'm a real bitch! And I know all good things come to an end. It's sad but it's true. I just want you to know, however this ends, for me, it was all worth it. You allowed me into your being, you allowed me to be a part of you, and for that, I'm grateful. I'm watching you sleep and you look so peaceful. I want to just come over there and rub my pussy over your entire body. I want to wake you up and demand that you make love to me! I haven't done it yet, but I want your dick in my mouth... I want to caress your balls and rub your manhood all over my face! Would that make me less than a woman? Would you respect me in the morning? Would you, Chandar, return the favor??? Yes, I want to be your freak, boo. I also want to be so much more. I would love to be Mrs. Grant... I would love to be your baby's mother... I would love to, uh oh, you're awake! I hope you don't think I'm crazy! You said the other night to Inf that you think you're in love... Was you serious? Maybe I'm in love also, because I was told love makes you do crazy things.*

*Hugs & Kisses Boo xxxooo*
*Karen*

By the time Chandar finished reading the letter, Karen was either knocked out, or she pretended to be asleep. Chandar scooted over and grabbed the pen… He had to write a response.

*Dear Karen,*

*A brother is truly blessed just to be in your presence. You're a good woman! Honestly, I haven't felt this good since I lost my best friend three years ago. After her, I thought I'd never love again, but now I'm forced to reconsider. Now I'm forced to evaluate the fact that a man can't control the way he feels.*
*No, I don't think you're insecure. You're a woman who understands the mechanics of life. Anyone who is willing to love is volunteering to be hurt. Love hurts! When you care for someone deeply and passionately, you inherit their pain. When they hurt, you hurt. When they're disappointed, it affects you. And when, not if, when, they're taken away from you… It crushes you. I guess you expressed it best when you said, 'all good things come to an end'. This is so true, but guess what? I'm not a freak for pain, but I'm once again willing to endure pain if this is the consequence of being with you. I'm feeling you, Karen! Don't laugh, but when I make love to you, sometimes I feel like crying! And I'm hardly what you would call an emotional person. You of all people should know that.*
*And please Karen, I'm begging you… If you want the dick in your mouth, by all means, take it there! Caress the balls and allow your tongue to explore the length of the snake! Will I return the favor? You damn skippy! Don't play with me, Karen! My dick is getting hard just thinking about sucking the juices from your pussy. As far as you being Mrs. Grant, I'm not making any promises, but anything is possible. I think I would enjoy that, but only time will tell. I do know that I would love for you to bear my child, because you would be an excellent mother. Let*

143

*us play our cards right and see what happens. Oh yeah… When I told Inf that I think I'm in love, I was very much serious.*

*Holla back!*

*Chandar*

Chandar cuddled up next to Karen and fell asleep.

Jerome Smith and his entourage were walking along Howard Hughes Parkway on some bullshit! They were about ten deep, and every one of them seemed to have a 'fuck the world' attitude. They were in Vegas for the weekend!

Jerome wanted to do some gambling but he didn't want to go back to MGM Grand, because he and his boys had damn near stomped a nigga to death in the hotel lobby earlier that evening.

So they found their way to Sweet Dreams. They were up in the spot stunting.

"Cuz I got on over a hundred thousand dollars' worth of jewelry! The night you break me, Rockefeller gonna have to come back from the grave and put his bank with yours!" Khalif said, shaking the dice. He was talking to Calvin Goodrich! Everybody knew how Calvin got the last name Goodrich… That niggaz money was longer than the Golden State Bridge.

"Just roll the dice, fat-boy," Calvin said.

They were playing cee-low!

"Hey, S.P.? Come get Calvin good and rich! When I finish with his little ass he's gonna be good and broke," Khalif yelled still shaking the dice before finally letting them bounce across the table.

"Tracey," Calvin said happily. Tracey was the slang for three. They got that from the word trey.

"If I can't get over a bitch, then you deserve to take my money," Calvin continued.

"What you roll, Khalif?"

"That nigga rolled a three," Calvin shouted.

"5 thousand, you don't four and better," Khalif challenged.

"No bet," Calvin said shaking the dice. For some reason, he didn't feel it.

"I'll take that bet," S.P. said.

Calvin rolled the dice until he got his point, which was a two.

"Ill doo-doo! Give me my money," Khalif yelled. He did a little fat man dance. Doo-doo was the slang for a two. They got that from the word duce.

"Parlay cuz. Bet it all back," Calvin suggested.

"Nope," Khalif said scooping up his money and then continued. "I'm going over there to play poker with Rome."

"Petty ass nigga! Come on S.P., what's your bet," Calvin challenged.

"What's in your bank," S.P. asked.

"Twenty-five grand."

"Oh, that's stopped! Bet it all Cousin."

Chandar was making his rounds through the casino. He

had just received a very disturbing call from Jerry Moore. Don Chi-Chi was murdered, and for some reason, the homie thought he had something to do with it.

*'This fool, Jerry Moore, done lost his mind! If I was gonna kill Don Chi-Chi, why the fuck would I follow him around?'*

Chandar placed a call to the homie Shan Will. Shan Will was in semi-retirement. He was striving to be a good Muslim and a father to his daughter, Arianna. What people failed to realize was you can take a man out the city, but you can't take the city out the man! Shan Will was an official gun busta... This half pint size dude would bust his gun at an all-time high! While Shan Will was trying to chill, there was a hurricane brewing inside him. If unleashed, niggaz would be in trouble! The phone call from Chandar opened the door.

"Ayo! Shan Will?"

"Who's this?"

"It be that ghetto star for real!"

"Oh, drama! Chandar, what's poppin'," Shan Will said and continued. "To what do I owe this phone call?"

"I need a favor."

"And that would be?"

"I need you to breeze through New York and hold down Jerry Moore for me. Keep that nigga out of trouble and make sure he's safe. I think that fool is going crazy!"

Shan Will was silent on the line.

"I also need you to be my eyes and ears. If there was someone else I could trust I would've called them... I need you homie!"

"Say no more!" Shan Will felt obligated to hold the

homies down. When he needed them, they were there! It was time to return the favor.

Chandar was walking past the security room when he noticed the door ajar. Sweet Dreams' personnel weren't even allowed in that room, only those with clearance.

Chandar entered the room and found two police officers with the Chief of Security staff studying the monitors.

"Is everything okay here?"

Sam, the Chief of Security, glanced in Chandar's direction.

"They're looking for some guys who assaulted a man at the MGM Grand."

"Take a look at these," one of the officers said, passing Chandar a stack of photos. Chandar examined the pictures carefully, and then passed them back to the cop.

"Recognize any of the faces?"

"Can't say that I do," Chandar responded and then continued, "Sam, if you need me, I'll be on the floor."

Chandar observed his normal pace and demeanor, but gradually made his way to the poker table where Rome was.

"Playboy, you got a few officers monitoring the cameras… They have pictures of you and your boys. If you're trying to leave the casino a free man, listen to me closely. There's a personnel service room down the hall from the restroom, it will lead you to the Philmore Hotel. Warn your boys, but be smooth about it. Leave your chips on the table, that will give the impression that you're coming back. Tell your boys to do the same." And Chandar kept it moving. He didn't have to tell Jerome twice.

When Chandar was living in the 'hood', he hated the police! Some things would never change!

# Chapter Nineteen

When Jerry Moore received the phone call from Mr. Kopell advising him that the K500 was ready for delivery, the big homie was euphoric! He instructed Mr. Kopell to have the car delivered to Denise's parents' house in Brownsville.

Jerry Moore and Denise were in the basement apartment counting money. The big homie was eager to exhaust their first supply of drugs because he planned on buying a big house out on Long Island. But for now, it was all about the grind.

The big homie's new recruit, Sarah, had Baisley on smash! Jerry Moore was amazed by how efficient she was as a business woman. She divided the day into three 8 hour shifts; 12am-8am, 8am-4pm, and 4pm-12pm. This ensured that the manufactured goods was available consistently, 24 hours a day. The crack filled bags were hermetically sealed, and this prevented the workers from tampering with the product. And Sarah prohibited her workers from taking loose change or one dollar bills, the customers needed to bring exact cash! If they had a ten dollar bill, they were given two nickels of crack… If they had a twenty dollar bill, they were given four nickel bags of crack. Sarah did this to limit the amount of time it took to complete a transaction. Her motto was: "Cop and go!"

The twins on 112th and Guy R. Brewer took a more liberal approached to their hustle, and when business picked up, Jerry Moore knew he would more than likely have to intervene. They broke the day down into two 12 hour shifts. Teddy took one shift and Eddie took the other! They cooked the work themselves, they bagged it up themselves, and they sold it themselves; they were doing hand to hand combat! The twins had no rules. They took currency in all denominations; dollar bills, quarters, dimes, nickels and even pennies. To them, money was money!

On The Bully, Cue had set up shop on three different blocks and had already established a day shift and night shift. He had yet to restrict the other hustlers from grinding, but he was selling fat nickel bags of crack, buy one get one free! That alone was putting a major dent in the smaller operations.

All Jerry Moore had to do was sit back and count his money. But after a while, he was reminded that counting money was a tedious job!

When Jerry Moore and Denise finally took a break from counting stacks, Denise jetted upstairs to see what her mom was cooking. When she came back down to the basement, she had a plate of food for the big homie, and a letter that the mailman had dropped off.

"Look Jerry, somebody wrote you from USP Canaan!"

Jerry Moore took the letter and looked at the return address. It was from his boy, Yahya Ruhani. Yahya was one of the few people he gave his information to before he left the penitentiary. He put the mail to the side and punished the fried fish, baked macaroni and cheese, and collard greens that Denise's mother made. After guzzling down a Hawaiian Punch, the big homie let out a loud belch and opened up the letter. It was short and to the point.


*Peace Big Homie,*

*I fast and pray that I'm not imposing on you, I know you*

*probably have a dozen things you'd rather be doing instead of reading this letter, so I'll strive to be brief.*

*Everything in here is basically the same; the struggle continues! I heard about the party they threw for you. I guess it's safe to say that the streets still have love for Jerry Moore! The question is, does Jerry Moore still have love for the streets?*

*You're always telling me that I'm facetious, and that most of my remarks be sarcastic... I ask, how else do I get the attention of a soldier who continuously places himself on a path of self-destruction? How else do I convey to a soldier that he's fighting the wrong war? Banging for the wrong side??? The two forces are good and evil. Who you with?*

*Never the less, I didn't write to preach to you. I actually just wanted to wish you well. Get with Chandar... He's moving in the right direction! When you were down, he was there for you. Where were all those other people who attended your party when 30 years in confinement was your reality? Keep your head straight soldier, we need good men like you out there... Don't promote recidivism! When time permits, holla back!*

*FAM 4 LIFE,*

*Yahya Ruhani*

Jerry Moore folded the letter up and placed it back in the envelope. He tore off the return address and handed it to Denise.

"When you go out, stop by the post office and get a thousand dollar money order made out to this name. Put that information on the back of it and send it to the address in Iowa."

The big homie had deep respect for Yahya. He was a good dude, and he never held back any punches.

To occupy his mind, Jerry Moore did a thousand pushups and fifteen hundred crunches while he waited for Tank and

Reggie Ransom to come and get him.

He showered and put on a white Sean John outfit. The sweater had a hood that he put over his head. The big homie had a lot on his mind!

When the doorbell rung, he patted Denise on the ass and told her to *keep it tight* before he bounced out the crib. He tossed Tank the keys to the K500 and instructed Reggie Ransom to sit up front. Jerry Moore had his game face on… Their intended destination was The Bully. Tank grabbed a couple of CD's from his car and they were ready to roll.

The K500 was grey with burgundy interior! There were TV's in the headrest and a 13 inch flat screen that dropped from the ceiling. There was wood throughout the dashboard, and the seats were butter soft leather; the two in the back boasted reclining capabilities.

Tank put in B.I.G.'s double CD and the slain rapper's voice came through the surround sound system crystal clear.

**'What's beef? Beef is when you need two gats to walk the street…'**

The K500 floated through the streets of New York with both style and grace.

**'Beef is when you roll no less than thirty deep…'**

Jerry Moore watched as the streets passed by quickly, and he was forced to ponder on the words of Yahya.

**'Beef is when I see you, guaranteed to be in ICU."**

They pulled up in front of Feasters on 116th Avenue and Supthin Boulevard. A young kid was standing outside posted up. Jerry Moore allowed his window to glide down.

"Shorty, come 'ere!" The Big Homie barked.

151

Peanut walked closer to the stretch Mercedes Benz.

"What you out here doing, hustling?"

"Yeah, yeah."

"Who you hustling for?"

"Big Time and Kool-Aid," Peanut reluctantly responded.

"You hear me? Get the fuck off this block before you disappear like Chuck! And tell that nigga, Big Time, he better stop putting work on my strip."

Jerry Moore pushed a button and the window glided up.

Tank pulled off, and the next time they stopped, they were on 115th Road. Cue was standing outside writing something in his little pad.

"Hey Cue! Get in the car," Reggie Ransom advised. Cue came around to the other side and got in next to big homie.

"How's business," Jerry Moore inquired.

"It's picking up," Cue said consulting his notepad before continuing. "The night shift pulled in 18,000 last night compared to 11,000 the night before."

"Dammit man! Tank drive to Baisley." Tank pulled away from the curb smoothly. Jerry Moore was in deep thought. Yahya had said, *'Get with Chandar... When you were down, he was there!'* This was very true.

*'Maybe Chandar didn't kill Don Chi-Chi,'* Jerry Moore thought. If nothing else, Chandar was a gangsta! If he killed Don Chi-Chi himself, or had him killed, why would he deny it?

Tank pulled behind Jerry Moore's white S600. The big homie pulled out a set of keys with the Mercedes Benz emblem on them. He passed them to Cue.

"Merry Christmas, homie!" Cue's eyes were as big as

saucers!

"Noooo! Are you serious? I mean, it's not even December," Cue said excitedly.

Jerry Moore did a brief rendition of Sade. "Every day is Christmas, and every night is New Year's Eve."

He rubbed Cue's head. "Reggie, go 'head and roll with Cue! I gotta meet Gino and Bugsy at the studio. Y'all fools be safe and I'll catch up with y'all later."

Del Gibson was tapping keys on his two-way pager when Jerry Moore entered studio 'B'. Ever since Del got back in contact with Ericka, the big dawg was on some real lovey dovey shit. He and Ericka would text message to each other all day long, and when they weren't sending text messages, they were talking on the phone; and when they weren't talking on the phone, they were together! Fuck what you heard, big dawgs needed love too!

Gino and Bugsy were already in the middle of a session, and Willie Black from the 4-1-0 Hustlers was also in the room, as was Maxwell Smart and a female engineer name Tiara. Willie Black was making a special guest appearance on Jerry Moore's mixtape.

Jerry Moore was proud of G-Bundles and Bugsy, he really underestimated their talent. He knew if their project went well, that he would be able to hold his own in the music industry. He would probably need to think about starting his own label, because he needed to be the captain of his own ship. He wanted to be able to promote a little friendly competition against Del Gibson and Loud Mouth Records. He wanted to compete against the other young, black, and rich entrepreneurs like Jermaine "Jaquan" Dawkins, CEO of Incognito Enterprise, and Rafi

"Husain" Moreno, CEO of Heartbeat Entertainment.

Jerry Moore had big goals, and being in someone else's shadow was not one them!

Jerome Smith and his team's weekend in Las Vegas had been cut short by that stunt they pulled at the MGM Grand. They were forced to catch an early flight back to New York.

As soon as they got in the city, Blueberry-Loc got in contact with Rome… He had some more work for him. Jerome was actually happy about that, because he had lost close to fifteen grand at the poker table in Sweet Dreams.

Nasty Nate breezed through 121 and Supthin to scoop Jerome up… He told Jerome to drive. Nasty Nate was a loner, he didn't really like doing jobs with other people. But if he had to work with somebody, he preferred to work with Jerome Smith.

They drove to Merrick Boulevard and made their way to the huge parking lot in front of the Soul Convention.

When the studio session was over, Jerry Moore, Gino, and Bugsy were leaving. Jerry Moore heard Del Gibson instructing Simoya, his receptionist, to send ten dozen roses somewhere. The big homie smiled; he was happy for Doctor Hyde!

When they stepped outside the Soul Convention, they had no idea they were walking into an ambush! Blueberry-Loc was taking the game to another level!

The black van crept to the curb, and the sliding door on the side of the van glided open. Nasty Nate was wearing a Jamaican hat that made it look like he had long dreads. He leveled the MP5 and smirked before pulling the trigger! The fully automatic machine gun jerked in his hands and fired high, shattering the glass above the entrance doors of the Soul Convention!

G-Bundles dove on top of Jerry Moore, pushing him out of harm's way! When Nasty Nate got full control of the MP5 and brought the barrage of bullets lower by aiming at the ground, he blazed fifteen to twenty holes in Bugsy! The homie was laid out on the ground!

Gino pulled out a black 21 shot nine millimeter and returned fire!

Nasty Nate retreated into the van, but Jerome was holding him down squeezing off shots from a Desert Eagle. One of the bullets found its mark and spun Gino around! Jerome threw the van in drive and peeled off! **SKIRRRRRRRRR!!!**

"Big homie, you alright," Gino asked, holding his shoulder. Blood was seeping through his fingers!

"No doubt! Let's get the fuck out of here!"

It was as if Tank was on the same page! He pulled up in the K500 and began beeping the horn. Jerry Moore ran over to Bugsy to see if he was alive.

"Damn," the big homie grunted. Then he and Gino jumped in the Benz and Tank peeled off. **SKIRRRRRRRRR!!!**

# Chapter Twenty

The Galaxy Intercontinental Business Jet landed at Kennedy Airport in New York City, and was directed to hanger 19. Chandar, Karen, Infrared, and Chandar's protégé, Jeff White, CEO of Colossal Publishing, made their way through the busy airport, to the street, where a stream of cabs waited.

Chandar had received a disturbing phone call from A-Blood, who conveyed that a threat had been made on Jerry Moore's life. Chandar was furious! All the valuable time and energy he used, not to mention money, trying to get Jerry Moore's conviction overturned, and now this dude was bugging the fuck out, throwing rocks at the penitentiary, and looking for a plot at a respectable graveyard.

Chandar was fed up, and he wasn't about to stand by and watch his friend throw his life away. Here he was again, being dragged backwards! If Jerry Moore wasn't one of the few people that Chandar counted as being a friend, Chandar would've kept his black ass in Nevada. He hated the crabs in a pot mentality of people in the ghetto!

Chandar finally made it out… He was gone! He did it! He defeated the odds and was able to move out of the 'hood. Now he found a woman that he was willing to sacrifice for, he was willing to try again to love… to trust.

'*What the hell could Jerry Moore possibly be thinking,*' he thought as the cab he and Karen were in sped through the streets of Queens. Chandar was dropping Karen off at her restaurant, and then he was meeting up with his team at the suite he kept on reserve at the Holiday Inn.

Karen noticed a slight change in Chandar's demeanor. For her entire stay in California and Nevada, Chandar was in high spirits and was virtually stress-free. After the phone call that he received from A-Blood, he was behaving as if someone died.

Karen just gave him his space, and prayed that everything was okay. Chandar wanted to drop her off at her home in Forest Hills, but Karen insisted she stop by her restaurant. She had been gone for over two weeks, and although she was positive her sister did a good job managing her business, she still couldn't wait to be sure.

After dropping Karen off, Chandar directed the cab to his mother's house in the East New York section of Brooklyn. He had a black Yukon Denali that he kept parked in front of his mother's property. His sister Pauline would drive the truck occasionally, but other than that, it was only used when Chandar was in town when he wasn't driving his Porsche.

He used his keys to deactivate the alarm and climbed up into the truck. He made his way to the hotel, calling the suite when he was 5 minutes away. Wild Blood answered the phone.

"Yo!"

"Wild Blood! Y'all fools get ready and meet me downstairs."

"We on our way!"

"Who's all there with you?"

"Everybody! O' Corleone, Makavelli, Shan Will, Infrared, and your man, Jeff."

"Alright, listen. I got the truck. So you, Inf, and Jeff can ride with me. Tell Makavelli to take Corleone and Shan Will with him in the Range. I'm getting off the highway right now."

Vinnie passed Doctor Hyde a cup of water. Del Gibson was yelling and screaming so much that his voice was getting hoarse. Everyone was walking on eggshells! Everyone except for A-Blood.

Del Gibson was heated because his studio was under scrutiny. Homicide detectives were crawling all over the place and they were asking too many damn questions. Del Gibson didn't blame A-Blood, but it was on the strength of A-Blood that Doctor Hyde gave Jerry Moore a position as an A&R.

No one in the room actually knew exactly what took place, but what they did know was that an artist who was recording in the dungeon was gunned down in less than 5 minutes after leaving the studio. Bugsy was pronounced dead on the scene!

Del Gibson hated the police! Furthermore, he didn't need them up in his business prying and digging. He was scared of what they might find.

The Chief Executive was drilling Rashid Triplett, In House Counsel, when Chandar and Infrared entered Loud Mouth Records' reception area. Simoya informed her boss of their presence, and moments later they were buzzed in.

"A-Blood, what the hell is going on," Chandar asked as he entered the conference room.

"Nobody knows," A-Blood responded, giving Chandar and Infrared dap before he continued. "The big homie said a black van pulled up out front, and a nigga with dreads opened fire on them. They killed the little homie, Bugsy."

"Where Jerry Moore at," Chandar asked.

"He's in Baisley laying low. Somebody gave the police a description of him, and they're looking for him for questioning."

Del Gibson came over with his signature scowl on his face. He wanted to know if there were any new developments regarding what happened.

"Negative," A-Blood said and continued. "Del, this is the homie, Chandar. Chandar, this is who I was telling you about for years. I'm sorry y'all have to meet this way."

Chandar stuck his hand out. Doctor Hyde hesitated, but then reached out and gave Chandar a firm handshake.

"It's good to finally meet you, Doctor Hyde."

"The feeling is mutual," Del said and then continued. "You have to excuse my attitude, but my business is at stake! This shit got me pissed the fuck off!"

"That's understandable, playboy. I'd probably feel the same way."

"And A-Blood, you know I love you, but I can't keep your boy on my payroll. The car is his, I'm not even sweating that, but please... Tell him to stay away from the studio."

They left the Soul Convention with basically the same information they had when they went in; nothing! Chandar was frustrated, but he was being patient.

He navigated his Yukon past Baisley with Makavelli driving close behind him. They went past 112th and Guy R. Brewer, and cruised The Bully looking for clues as to what the hell was going on.

Chandar was driving past the new projects on 121 and

Supthin when he thought he saw a familiar face. He didn't know why, but he pulled over and double parked... Makavelli followed suit.

There was a group of people posted up in front of the buildings. And judging from their blue bandanas, they were more than likely Crips.

Chandar jumped out of his truck, and his team was on automatic, they were right there with him. The only ones strapped were Wild Blood and Shan Will.

As Chandar and his team approached the group, the environment became hostile, and a couple of the Crips began reaching and pulling out hardware.

Fuck what you heard, Shan Will was reaching too, but Chandar stopped him! He had found the familiar face that he spotted... It was the face of Jerome Smith!

"What's cracking," Jerome said aggressively, either not remembering or not recognizing Chandar.

Shan Will was a loose cannon! "What's poppin'," he shot back.

Niggaz from the Crips were now openly pointing guns at Chandar and his team. The visiting team was clearly outnumbered!

"Playboy, take a look at my face! You can't possibly smoke that much weed," Chandar said in the face of adversity.

Jerome took a closer look, and then it dawned on him! "Las Vegas? You the one who helped me duck the law?"

Chandar smiled. "Bingo!"

"Y'all niggaz put them mutha fucking guns down," Jerome yelled. Calvin Goodrich, S.P., Khalif, and the rest of their squad began lowering their guns. "I said put the fucking

guns away," Jerome snapped, and then continued. "Come on, let's walk and talk."

Jerome and Chandar strolled up the block. Both teams lingered in the cut, not far behind.

"The name is Jerome!"

"Chandar."

"That was good looking out at the casino. If it wasn't for you, I probably wouldn't be here right now."

"That wasn't about nothing, playboy! The pigs are the real enemy!"

"That's true," Jerome said and then continued. "And I do smoke a lot of weed, but what made you stop by... What brought you to this part of town?"

"I don't know... I wanna say instinct."

"Okay, but you still had to have a purpose."

"Listen, I'm gonna share an idea with you... If you like it, you can get involved. And if you don't, just forget about it."

"I'm listening."

"I wanna start a movement. Everybody knows that war isn't beneficial for nobody in most instances, so I came up with an idea to move toward peace as oppose to always moving toward war... At least when it comes to the red and blue! The name of the movement is CABBAGE! C.A.B.B.A.G.E. is an acronym that stands for Crips and Bloods Banging Against Gang Enmity. I think with the right leadership, we can do big things for our people... especially the youth."

"What is the movement supposed to consist of? I mean, what role will the Crips play in this?"

"We can start it as a basketball tournament, similar to

161

B.A.K.E, Brother Against Killing Each other. We'll put together Crip teams and Blood teams to demonstrate that we can co-exist and get along without fighting and shooting each other."

"I don't know! We got this dude, Jerry Moore, setting up shop across the street. He's a Blood! He's literally taking food off of my people's plate. Sooner or later, this may cause a war."

"Is that your only concern?"

"That I can think of,"

"That won't be a problem! His boys will be off that block before the sun goes down!"

"If what you say is true, I'm with you 100%!"

"Give me a couple of days and I'll get back with you."

"That's what's up!"

# Chapter Twenty One

Jerry Moore came out of building 4 in Baisley Projects and surveyed the area. The big homie was on point! He wore a Teflon bulletproof vest under two oversized white tees, and his baggy jeans had pockets deep enough to conceal the 40 caliber handgun he was toting. Somebody wanted the big homie dead, and he wasn't taking the threat lightly!

Jerry Moore's red and white GSX1000 sat idle in front of the building. He put the key in the ignition and turned it to the right before pushing the start button. The powerful engine instantly roared to life. The big homie took the helmet off the handlebars and put it on as he straddled the bike. A small amount of pressure from the left foot, while holding the clutch, was enough to put the bike in first gear. Jerry Moore revved the throttle and popped the clutch, briefly launching the rocket on wheels into the air. He maneuvered through the projects before leaping off the curb and hauling ass down Guy R. Brewer Boulevard toward 112th Avenue.

When he got to 112th, he noticed that the block was cluttered. Hood rats were standing around trying to look cute like the block was a runway. Broke ass niggas were passing around 40's of Olde English like that shit was cool. Crack heads were lingering on the block and neither Teddy nor Eddie was anywhere to be found.

When you hit 112th, coming from Baisley, you make a

right turn and you're on the strip. The strip was actually a dead end block, so when you drove in, there was only one way out. Jerry Moore lifted his helmet on top of his head so the people could see who he was, and he cruised into the block.

Everybody was breaking their necks trying to get a glance at the nigga who virtually overnight had the whole hood on lock!

The big homie spotted Teddy sitting on a porch in front of a green house, so he rode up on the sidewalk and parked the bike. As soon as he pulled up, he noticed the peculiar smell of crack and weed in the air. The shit must've been good, because Teddy still had the blunt smoking in his hand!

"What's up, big homie," Teddy said as if everything was sweet. Jerry Moore approached smoothly and slapped the shit out of the little nigga.

"Ma-fucker, you're getting' high?" Before Teddy could recuperate, Jerry Moore snatched him with one hand and slapped the shit out of him again! "You're over here smoking my shit! Where's my money, nigga?"

"I got it big homie! I got it all!"

"Where your product at," Jerry Moore demanded.

"It's stashed on the side of the house, big homie. Please man, just let me show you! It's all there."

Jerry Moore shoved him real hard! "It better be!"

Teddy scrambled to the side of the house to retrieve his package. Anybody with sense would've kept running without looking back… This nigga was too scared to run! He brought back the brown paper bag holding his stash. Jerry Moore snatched it out of his hands and began to analyze the red crack filled bags. They were skimpy like a mother fucker… Teddy was tapping the merchandise!

"Nigga, you stealing from me," Jerry Moore said walking toward Teddy.

Teddy was backing up, looking like he was finally ready to run. By now, there was an audience watching.

Jerry Moore pulled out the 40 cal. from his pants pocket and aimed it at Teddy.

"You better not run! Where's the rest of my shit?"

"It's… It's in the house, man. Please, big homie, don't kill me! I got a daughter."

Jerry Moore reached out quickly, grabbed him by the shirt, and began bashing him in the face with the gun. Teddy was on the ground bleeding!

"Don't have my shit when I come back through here tonight, you and your brother gonna be missing just like Chuck!"

Jerry Moore put the gun back in his pocket, got on his bike, and hauled ass off the strip.

On the strength of Chandar, Cue ordered his workers to leave 121st Avenue and Supthin Boulevard. They relocated to 119th and Supthin, and it was business as usual.

Cue stood on 115th Avenue and Supthin Boulevard, his white S600 Mercedes parked at the curb. Shan Will was posted up in front of the barbershop, as was Big Rock… They were holding Cue down! Big Rock weighed close to 300 pounds and looked as if he could kill a man with his bare hands. Shan Will was a short dude, but he carried cannons he called equalizers. He described it best when he said, "A little nigga with a big gun makes everybody the same size."

Cue was playing with numbers in his pocket size pad

when Jerry Moore rode up on the sidewalk with his bike. The big homie broke the bike down and killed the engine, taking off his helmet and putting it on the handlebars.

"Big homie, what's poppin'," Cue said, walking up to Jerry Moore and giving him some dap.

Shan Will was really on point now! Niggaz had tried to kill the big homie, but as long as Shan Will was around, he was determined not to let anything happen to him.

"Shan Will, fuck is up my nigga," Jerry Moore said, smiling out of respect for the soldier.

"I'm just chilling! It's all about you for-real, for-real. I'm here out of loyalty!"

Jerry Moore was glad Shan Will came through! He needed gangstaz like Shan Will around him at all times. That would make niggaz think twice about acting stupid.

"Big Rock, how are you," the big homie asked. He actually came out to boost the morale of the troops. Niggaz tried to get at the general, but that shit wasn't about nothing!

"I'm maintaining, gangsta… you know I got your back," Big Rock replied.

"Cue, let me hold the keys to your whip. Come on y'all, let's go for a ride," the big homie said. He was sending a message to the hood; gangstas don't hide!

Cue tossed him the keys to the Benz, and Jerry Moore went around and jumped into the driver's seat. Shan Will jumped in the front with Jerry Moore, and Big Rock got in the back.

Jerry Moore made a U-turn and headed down The Bully; but unfortunately, a marked police cruiser was in the vicinity and observed the illegal U-turn. The cops followed the Mercedes a few blocks, calling in the plate number before putting on flashing lights and pulling them over.

Jerry Moore had Jay-Z's *The Takeover* banging in the system, and he pulled over real nonchalant, like he wasn't carrying a gun.

"You know I'm strapped, right," Shan Will asked looking to the big homie for direction.

"Me too," was the big homie's simple response.

The officer took his time approaching. When he got to the window, he demanded, "Turn the music down!"

Jerry Moore looked at the cop arrogantly. "Since when is it against the mother fucking law to listen to music," he shot back. Still, he reached over and lowered the volume on the CD player.

"Oh, you're a smart ass! License and registration!"

Jerry Moore reached up to the sun visor and passed the registration and insurance to the cop. Then he reached in his pocket and handed over his license.

"This nigga don't know who the fuck I be," the big homie said to Shan Will.

"Excuse me," the black officer asked.

"Why you stop me," Jerry Moore shot back.

"Because you made an illegal U-turn, and you're driving without wearing a seatbelt!"

"Well, write me a ticket and let me get the fuck out of here!"

The officer looked at Jerry Moore long and hard. Then he went and sat in his patrol car for what seemed like forever. Shan Will knew right then and there that Chandar spoke the truth when he said Jerry Moore done went crazy.

When the officer came back, he passed the big homie his ticket.

"This is a nice car Jerry Moore! Enjoy it while you can."

While the cop was walking away, Jerry Moore was tearing up the ticket. He tossed it out the window and pulled away from the curb.

Officer Bennett was back at the precinct discussing the arrogant man in the Mercedes with a fellow officer when Detective Peppy from Homicide Division butted in the conversation.

"What did you say the guy's name was?"

"Moore... Jerry Moore!"

"That's the guy we're looking for! We need to question him about the shooting that took place at the Soul Convention. Witnesses put him at the scene... He was with the guy who was killed."

"I'll tell you this. The guy was arrogant! Like he's untouchable or something,"

Peppy made a mental note to get with the Anti-Gang Unit... He was curious about this Jerry Moore character. He would do some research and see what he could come up with.

# *Chapter Twenty Two*

Tomorrow is promised to no one, and no one knows what tomorrow will bring! Everyone was being drawn to their fate.

It was a taste of déjà vu when Chandar was driving down Queens Boulevard, enroute to see his boo, and he noticed a Lexus truck behind him with flashing lights on the roof. He pulled over and was genuinely surprised to see Detective John O' Conner and Bill Doherty approaching his Porsche.

A blast from the past! Chandar hadn't seen these guys in over 3 years, since he paid them $50,000 to help him with a problem.

They both were at the driver's side door when Chandar pushed a button commanding the window to glide down.

"Well, well, well. If it isn't Chandar Grant, Nine Trey Gangsta! What brings you back to New York," John O' Conner said with a big shit eating grin on his face.

"Batman and Robin, how's it going," Chandar responded and then continued. "If I would've known I'd run into you guys, I would've brought some souvenirs of Las Vegas."

John O' Conner and Bill Doherty, AKA Batman and Robin, were filthy cops! They had a brigade of dirty cops working under them throughout the city. Everyday Internal Affairs was getting closer and closer to taking the network of bad cops down, and Batman and Robin blamed Chandar for that problem.

The dirty cops had their spot blown after trying to help Chandar get his girl back. William Cook had kidnapped Chandar's girl, Lisa, and her mother, because Lisa's brother, Lucky, had kidnapped William Cook's wife, Michelle. Lucky kidnapped Michelle to extort money from William Cook, but William Cook had a better idea. He kidnapped Lucky's mother and sister and demanded a fair exchange.

As a favor to Anthony Orena who was doing business with Chandar at the time, Batman and Robin intervened on behalf of Chandar… They tried to assure that the exchange was completed without incident. They failed! Things went haywire and over half a dozen people were killed, including Chandar's girlfriend, Lisa.

No one ever found out how William Cook knew where to find Lucky's family, but rumor was that it was a member of the Bloods that gave him that information.

That single incident left Internal Affairs with their noses so far up Batman and Robin's asses that they couldn't fart without it being reported.

"Screw you and your souvenirs, Chandar. You're going down," Bill Doherty yelled.

Chandar was taken aback! "I sense a lot of hostility coming from your partner John. Am I missing something here? Do I owe you guys some money or something?"

"You arrogant nigger," Bill said moving to snatch Chandar out of the car, but he was stopped by his partner.

"Calm down Bill, let me handle this," John O' Conner said, playing the part of Chandar's savior, and then continued. "You made it bad for us a few years ago, Chandar. All the money in the world, let alone the measly $50,000 you gave us, would've been worth what we went through… What *we're going* through. The incident at the train yards caused us to lose our stripes! Our own people don't trust us anymore! We're being monitored! Internal Affairs wants to take us down and they won't stop until they do. Now we're getting messages that your crew is back in New York. They say *Lucky* is back in New York! This is like a slap in the face! Things seemed to be cooling down for us, and now it's heating up all over again."

These were new revelations for Chandar. He knew it was crazy that night at the train yards, and Batman and Robin were a little reserved when they came to collect their money, but he didn't know it was that bad for the dirty cops. After all, it was their idea to fake Lucky's death, and the explosion was *their* idea, but Chandar played the sympathy card.

"I'm sorry to hear that John, I really am. I didn't know things got that bad for you guys… I was busy mourning my daughters' mother."

"And we're sorry about *that*," Bill said sarcastically. Chandar let it pass.

"Is there anything I can do, John? Do you guys need some money?"

"Keep your money, Chandar! If you really want to help, go back to the west coast. If Jerry Moore is smart, he'll go back with you."

That last comment caught Chandar's attention. "What does Jerry Moore have to do with this?"

"Jerry Moore's' days are numbered! Either someone is going to kill him, or he's going back to prison. The way I see it, he better be happy if we get to him first."

Nasty Nate and Jerome were up to their old tricks again. They never tried to kill Jerry Moore! They were paid to kill everyone close to Jerry Moore. But the catch was Jerry Moore had to be there to witness it.

That was Blueberry-Loc's attempt at causing psychological damage. Now, a week after the Soul Convention incident, he wanted Jerry Moore to be hurt… Not killed, but hurt real bad.

Nasty Nate and Jerome parked a block away from Denise's house! It was 4 AM, and Jerry Moore's bike was parked out front. They worked quickly and quietly sabotaging the big homie's motorcycle.

"That nigga gonna fuck around and kill his self," Nate said when they were back in the van.

"I hope so because I'm tired of playing these games," Jerome responded and then continued. "I'm starting to think something is seriously wrong with Blueberry-Loc. That nigga is weird!"

Chandar stopped by a supply store that specialized in printing and embroidery, and placed an order to make 60 t-shirts for the C.A.B.B.A.G.E. tournaments. He helped with the design and chose the different colors of the t-shirt.

The front of the t-shirt would have the acronym C.A.B.B.A.G.E. in a semi-circle going across the top. Under that would be two hands gripping each other in a handshake. On the wrist of the right hand would be a red bandanna, and on the wrist of the left hand would be a blue bandanna. The back of the t-shirt would display the meaning of C.A.B.B.A.G.E: Crips and Bloods Banging Against Gang Enmity. The colors would be basically blue and red, thirty of each.

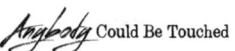 

Satisfied, Chandar gave the man a deposit and headed to pick up Jerry Moore.

One of Chandar's biggest challenges was trying to draw Jerry Moore into meaningful dialogue. Jerry Moore was making that hard because he was acting as if he couldn't trust anyone. Chandar resented Jerry Moore's attitude, but he refused to give up on his homie that easily.

He pulled up in front of Denise's house just as the big homie was coming out the door. Jerry Moore walked to the passenger side of the Porsche with his helmet in his hand, and Chandar pushed the button causing the window to glide down.

"Follow me! I'm taking my bike because I have to meet A-Blood uptown later on. Is that cool," Jerry Moore asked, as if he needed permission. Chandar got out the car and came around.

"You don't say what's up or nothing! You ain't happy to see me?" He embraced Jerry Moore and then continued. "We can't let shit change, homie! Without Jerry Moore, there is no Chandar... And without Chandar, there is no Jerry Moore! We made it to where we are by being down for each other, fool! We played team ball, good guy/bad guy! Let's take it back to what works... I got a surprise for you, too!"

Jerry Moore was listening. He wanted to trust Chandar. He wanted things to be like they use to be, but the big homie was paranoid! He still had his suspicions that Chandar was somehow involved with the incident at the Soul Convention. Jerry Moore was convinced that someone was trying to kill him, he just didn't know who.

"I got a lot on my mind, homie! I just need time to sort it all out, but you know it's all love. You my dawg!" he gave Chandar dap! Chandar grabbed the motorcycle helmet and told

Jerry Moore to take the car ... he wanted to ride the bike. Jerry Moore gave him the keys!

Inside the Porsche, Jerry Moore breezed through the selection of CD's and put on Beanie Sigel, *The Truth*. Chandar started up the bike, and Jerry Moore put the Porsche in first gear. Beanie Sigel's voice permeated the vehicle.

The big homie pulled off. Through the rearview mirror, he could see Chandar following him.

*Niggas wanna know if Beanie Sigel life is real,*

*Nigga twenty-five to life is real!*

*I get a body, take me right to jail...*

Jerry Moore was feeling the track! Beanie was painting a graphic picture that was painfully real. The Big Homie knew from experience.

*What you know about twenty-three and one*

*Locked down all day, underground, never seeing the sun?*

*Vision stripped from you, never seeing your son...*

When they stopped at the light, Chandar pulled up on the side of the Porsche. Jerry Moore rolled down the window.

"This shit feel kinda stiff, playboy. You might need a tune-up or something. Maybe change the oil," Chandar said.

*Tell me what your life like*

*Shit, mine is real*

*Everything signed and sealed...*

"This Porsche is driving smoother than a ma-fucker," Jerry Moore responded. The light turned green and he skidded off. **Skirrrr!!!**

Jerry Moore burned through second and third gear! He

174

was about to shift to fourth gear when he looked into the rearview mirror and saw Chandar take a spill! The bike was flipping like an acrobat, and Chandar was flying through the air!

Jerry Moore broke the Porsche down in record breaking time.

"Damn," he thought, getting out of the car. Chandar was face down in the middle of the street. Jerry Moore ran to his body! He wasn't moving.

"Chandaaar," the big homie yelled.

Chandar was either unconscious or dead, and the big homie was scared. It took a tragedy for Jerry Moore to finally realize how much he loved and cared for his homie.

Tomorrow is promised to no one, and no one knows what tomorrow will bring! Everyone was being drawn to their fate.

# Chapter Twenty Three

Members of the Narcotics Task Force sat idle in a blue van on 110th Avenue and Guy R. Brewer Boulevard. They were doing buy and bust set-ups since night fall and they had four people in back of the van handcuffed and sitting on the floor.

Crack head Calvin rarely made his way to this part of town, but he moved as if he knew his way around.

"Who working," he asked a group of young boys standing on the corner getting drunk.

The block was flooded! Cars were double parked, Nas was blasting from somebody's sound system talking about he made you look, and crack fiends were being directed to the porch of a green house in the middle of the block.

"Go see Teddy," one of the guys said pointing in the direction of the green house.

Crack head Calvin walked into the dead end block of 112th Avenue and found Teddy serving a pregnant woman. He waited his turn and then passed Teddy $10.00.

"Let me get 2 fat ones!"

The CB radio of the detectives in the blue van on 110th Avenue came to life.

"Team 'B' move in! Suspect is a black guy wearing a

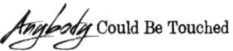 

dark t-shirt and white sneakers"

"Wow! He just described half the people in the vicinity," the detective driving the van yelled as he pulled away from the curb and headed toward 112th Avenue.

Team 'A' was already moving in! They ran down on the young guy on the corner who directed crack head Calvin to Teddy, and simultaneously with guns drawn they had Teddy hemmed up on the porch of the green house.

By the time the blue van appeared on the block, Teddy and his co-defendant were already handcuffed. His co-defendant was loaded in the van, but Teddy was thrown in back of an unmarked car.

The detectives in the car started the scare tactics early, and when Teddy started singing, they knew they hit the jackpot.

"You're going away for a long time boy, unless you do some quick talking. We got you dead right, so don't play stupid! Now, who you working for?"

Teddy didn't blink, and he didn't think twice. "The big homie... Jerry Moore!"

Del Gibson knew it was time for a change, but he truly didn't know if he was ready. The incident that happened in front of the Soul Convention showed him how fragile life could be. That could've easily been him out there!

There was an opportunity knocking at his door, and he decided to answer it. Doctor Hyde scoured the diamond district until he found what he was looking for.

Next, he called Ericka and told her to put on something nice, he was coming to get her. That was one of the things she loved about Del Gibson. He still had that thug quality, yet he was a gentleman, and he was so damn spontaneous.

He scooped Ericka up in his green CL600 Benz... He felt like driving tonight. They went to a cozy restaurant in Greenwhich Village. They ate shrimp, oysters, linguini in garlic and oil, and they drank wine.

The whole evening, Ericka couldn't help but think that something was up. She couldn't put her finger on it, but Del was acting strange.

When they left the restaurant, to Ericka's surprise, a horse and carriage was waiting on them. Del helped her up first and he followed. Ericka wondered what was going on.

They put the heavy blanket that smelled like the horses over their laps to protect them from the night breeze then they traveled toward Central Park! When they were about a block away from the park, they saw a man selling single roses.

"Let me buy the lady a rose," Del advised the driver of the horses. He pulled over near the man with the flowers.

"How much for a rose, sir," Doctor Hyde asked.

"Twenty dollars," the young black man responded with a smile. Del dug in his pockets and passed him a fifty.

"Give the lady a rose." The man passed Ericka a rose with a small box attached to it.

"Oh, thank you! This is so sweet," Ericka exclaimed. She smelled the rose and then fondled with the little box attached to it. When she opened it, she couldn't believe her eyes. She covered her mouth! "Oh my God,"

"I've been meaning to ask you something all night." Del took the 5 carat ring out of the box and grabbed Ericka by the hand. "Ericka, I'm deeply in love with you! I've wanted you ever since we worked together on Broad Street. It would make me a very happy man if you would do me the honor and be my wife."

Ericka was crying! "Yes, I will," she cried. "Yes, Del,"

"Congratulations, Mr. Gibson," the flower man yelled.

"Thanks Vinnie!"

Kool-Aid and Peanut were on the corner of 116th Avenue and Supthin Boulevard getting their grind on. The odds were against them! In addition to being on point for the police and stickup kids, they had to add Jerry Moore to the list of people to look out for. Kool-Aid really didn't give a fuck, but Peanut was smart enough to know when he didn't have any wins.

Big Time was laying low trying to plan his next move. He was still selling weight to a select few, but Jerry Moore was making it harder and harder for people to eat.

Crack head Ebony and another crack head looking dude approached Kool-Aid and Peanut. Peanut jumped at the chance to make a sale, but Kool-Aid was leery. He wasn't serving anybody he didn't know.

"Who's working," Ebony asked. Kool-Aid gave her a skeptical look. Ebony knew Kool-Aid had scary ways, so she spoke up.

"This is my cousin, y'all. He wants two," she lied. Peanut dug in his superman waistband underwear and pulled out 2 vials of crack.

Crack head Calvin passed him the marked ten dollar bill, and took the 2 vials before him and Ebony walked away.

Ebony didn't know crack head Calvin from a hole in a wall, but she co-signed for him because she wanted to get high.

The van came up on the sidewalk and detectives jumped out with guns drawn!

Kool-Aid and Peanut took off like runaway slaves! They split up and hit backyards, jumping over fences. The detectives were on Peanut's ass, but he was able to throw his stash. He jumped fences and ran through yards until he came out on the next block. He took off his New York Yankees fitted cap, and walked as if he was never running away from the Po-Po.

An unmarked car raced up the block, and crack head Calvin pointed Peanut out. The detectives jumped out and threw Peanut to the ground. They couldn't find his stash, but that was cool, because they had one to put on him, along with a defaced nine millimeter.

Peanut cried foul ball, but his cries fell on deaf ears; however, there was someone who was willing to listen when they reached the 113th precinct. He was from the homicide division, and his name was Peppy!

Peppy was kind to Peanut! All the other officers were behaving like savages who would do anything for a collar. This was the old good cop/bad cop routine but Peanut didn't peep game. He agreed to talk to Peppy.

"That's not my gun and those aren't my drugs! They planted that stuff on me," Peanut protested.

"I want to believe you, young man, but then there's still the marked ten dollar bill you were caught with."

Peanut was speechless. He looked at the homicide detective in defeat.

"Now... I can help you, but I need you to help me. Tell me what you know about Jerry Moore."

Peanut began to see a mirage! He thought he was seeing a way out of trouble... He began to make stuff up about Jerry

Moore to save himself.

"He took over The Boulevard. He supposed to be taking over the whole borough, and then he's going after Brooklyn!"

"This is good information, young man. But I'm interested in the more serious stuff, like murder."

Peanut was on automatic.

"He killed Chuck!"

"Chuck? You mean Charles Thomas?"

"Yeah! And he told me if I didn't wanna be missing like Chuck, I better not sell drugs on The Boulevard!"

"You're not shitting me, are you," Peppy yelled and slammed his hands against the table. He hit the jackpot!

"No! He even killed Chuck's brother and his nephews. It was in the newspaper, but they didn't know who did it!"

Peppy smiled. Jerry Moore was in serious trouble.

"Are you willing to testify to this?"

All Peanut wanted was to save himself, sucker ass nigga!

"Yes!"

# *Chapter Twenty-Four*

Karen drove her Cadillac Escalade to Jamaica Hospital at top speed! She was on the VanWyck Expressway doing a buck, who gives a fuck, smoking boom and the whole nine.

In the waiting area she found Ms. Grant and Pauline, and she rushed to them to offer support and find out Chandar's condition.

"I got here as quick as I could. How's he doing?"

"You don't worry about nothing baby. It's in the hands of the good Lord," Ms. Grant said trying to stay positive.

"They're running test on him now," Pauline added and then continued. "The doctor said he'll inform us of the results shortly."

"Chandar is a strong young man, you don't worry about nothing," Ms. Grant said rocking in her seat.

Jerry Moore came into the waiting room with two cold sodas. He gave one to Ms. Grant and one to Pauline.

"Karen, what's up? You want a soda or something," Jerry Moore asked. If Karen didn't know any better it looked as if Jerry Moore had been crying.

"No, I'm cool Jerry, thank you! Are you alright?"

"I'll be alright," the big homie responded, and took a seat next to Ms. Grant.

While they were waiting, Jerry Moore received a phone call from the Triple 'A' Auto Repair Shop. They were the ones that towed his motorcycle.

"Yo!"

"Yeah, I'm looking for a Mr. Jerry Moore, the owner of the wrecked GSX1000 we scraped up earlier today."

"This is he,"

"Okay, I have good news and bad news. What you want to hear first?"

"Give me the good news?"

"That one's easy... I can salvage your bike! It's gonna cost you, but I think we can make her like new."

"What's the bad news?"

"This is the hard one, but here we go... Either the morons who sold you your bike made a serious mistake, or someone is trying to kill you! Your bike was sabotaged."

Jerry Moore was stressed the fuck out, but he had one good reason to be happy. Chandar was okay! Ms. Grant, Pauline, and Karen were allowed in the room with him! They only allowed 3 visitors at a time, so someone had to wait downstairs. Jerry Moore opted to be the one because he wanted to talk to Chandar alone anyway.

A-Blood had called and said he was on his way, as was Infrared, Wild Blood, and Jeff White.

When Ms. Grant, Pauline, and Karen came downstairs, the big homie got on the elevator and went to the fifth floor. He hated hospitals almost as much as he hated prisons, because they seemed so cold, and it was as if death lingered in the air.

Jerry Moore found room 514. Chandar shared a room with an older black man who had suffered from a seizure. Just seeing his homie in a hospital bed brought Jerry Moore back to reality... They were both mortal! He understood right then and there that anybody could be touched! He humbly walked to the edge of the bed. Chandar had a busted lip, but other than that, he looked fine.

"Playboy, I think you need to get your oil changed," Chandar joked, referring to the motorcycle.

"You got jokes, huh? On a serious note, you scared me, Blood! For the first time in my life I'm ready to admit that I was scared."

"Is that right?"

"Dammit man! I thought you were dead! It took something like this to happen for me to realize we're family. I thought-" Jerry Moore took a deep breath! This was hard for him. "I thought you had Don Chi-Chi killed, and I thought... I was thinking it was you that was trying to kill me."

The room was silent. Chandar knew Jerry Moore still had things on his mind, so he waited for him to finish. "Whoever is trying to kill me sabotaged my bike. The guys who towed my bike confirmed that. I've been acting like a cold sucker towards you, and now you're laying in the hospital when it's supposed to be me," he said, looking Chandar dead in the eyes.

"Don't be so hard on yourself, big homie! I'm not tripping... I don't have time to trip, we need to find out who's trying to get at you, and we need to find out quick. Bottom line," Jerry Moore knew he played himself, and he was now prepared to let Chandar lead.

"I don't deserve to be called big homie, you're the real big homie! How do you feel?" Chandar smiled. "As long as I keep still, I'm cool! When I move, my body hurts like a ma-

184

fucker."

Jerry Moore and Chandar talked for about an hour. Chandar told his homie about the C.A.B.B.A.G.E. movement and made him commit to playing in the tournament. Jerry Moore asked about Karen, and Chandar admitted that he thought he was in love.

"You said you had a surprise for me," Jerry Moore said. As if on cue, A-Blood, Infra-red, Wild Blood, and Jeff White entered the room.

"Y'all know only 3 people supposed to be up here at a time, right," Chandar asked, mocking the rules.

"I told Wild Blood to wait downstairs," Inf said laughing.

"Fuck outta here," Wild Blood responded.

"Chandar, what happened fool? Don't tell me that I have to give you some more lessons on how to ride a motorcycle," A-Blood said.

"Playboy, I damn near killed myself! If it wasn't for the helmet, I probably wouldn't be here."

"Wow," Infra-red said.

"Yeah! The pressure from the fall knocked me out, I got a few bumps and bruises, but I'm okay. They want to run a few tests and I'm out of here in the morning."

"That's good news," Jeff White interjected.

"Speaking of good news… Jeff, tell Jerry Moore about the surprise," Chandar said with excitement.

"Well…" Jeff White started in a country drawl, and then continued. "I was thinking about starting a branch of Colossal Publishing in Atlanta, but… Chandar speaks very highly of you, big homie! I decided to start Colossal East right here in New

York, and I want you to be the captain of the ship. You don't need to know absolutely nothing about the publishing world, but you will need to hire people that do. You get to choose the location of the offices, and you'll be doing the hiring and firing... If you accept my offer, you answer to no one, but I'll be by your side the whole time to consult you."

Jerry Moore smiled. Chandar really had his back. "Dammit man! I wanna give it a shot! I have a few things to take care of first, but yeah, let's do it!"

In the following weeks, they got the C.A.B.B.A.G.E. tournaments off the ground. There was a little tension for the first few games, but eventually the Crips and Bloods began to loosen up around each other. It was amazing! They had good sportsmanship, and after the game, they gave each other love.

Never the less, there was one incident out of the whole tournament that turned into a tragedy. And although that was good considering the history of the two gangs, at the end of the day, someone was deprived of life.

What happened was Chandar and Jerome concluded that all referees would be neutral, because if they were Cuz or Blood, there was a chance that they would be one-sided.

During a playoff game, one of the refs name Ty was making terrible calls. It was like the guy was blatantly cheating. But what it most likely came down to was he really didn't know what he was doing!

It was two minutes left in the game and the Bloods were leading by 6 points. Ty made back to back bad calls that resulted in the game being tied, and the Crips ultimately won the game. Shan Will, in a fit of rage, grabbed a baseball bat from one of the kids playing stickball nearby, and ran up to Ty and batted him

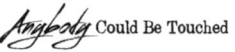 

down. It was strictly head shots!

Almost simultaneously, some knucklehead began shooting in the air! Reggie Ransom, G-Bundles, Infra-red, Wild Blood, Big Rock, Cue, and a host of Bloods formed a circle around Chandar and Jerry Moore! They formed a human force field! And the two ghetto stars were ushered to safety.

All in all, the C.A.B.B.A.G.E. movement was proving to be a good thing. Next on the agenda was a bus ride to Six Flags Great Adventures.

They were having gangsta parties and the days were sunny, but the forecast showed that a storm was approaching.

# Chapter Twenty-Five

Nasty Nate was laid back in the hotel room trying to see where Tara's head was at. I mean, she was giving him some head, but he was still trying to tap into her mental. To accomplish that, he kept Shorty with a seemingly unending supply of Purple Haze. They smoked as if they thought the world was coming to an end. And if this was so, they would be high when they died!

Whenever Nate got together with Tara, he would pump her for information. As a result, whenever Jerry Moore was with Lashawn, who just so happen to be Tara's best friend, Nate could pinpoint the whereabouts of the big homie.

"Ayo boo! What the fuck is cracking with your girlfriend, Lashawn? I told you my homie is tryin' to get at her. What you think *I* wanna fuck your friend or something," Nate was a manipulative dude.

"Boy, please! I'm not even worried about you fucking my friend. I told you, she fuck with the big homie! He got that bitch nose wide open."

"Fuck that nigga! He could suck a Crip dick! Tell your girl my cuz tryna holla. Matter of fact, call shorty right now and I'll call-"

"Are you listening to me? Jerry Moore is at her house right now, I just finished talking to Lashawn! I told you, I got you. I'm gonna try to hook something up, but it's up to her. I can't make her do nothing."

'*Shut the fuck up bitch*,' Nate thought. He already heard what he needed to hear.

It was nothing but dimed out bitches, about 6 of them! They were wearing thongs and cut off t-shirts as they washed cars by hand.

Blueberry-Loc watched as they washed his baby blue 645 BMW. He adjusted the brown snake as he felt it reacting to the beautiful ladies.

'*These bitches is bad, every last one of 'em*,' Blueberry-Loc thought as he watched the platinum Carrera GT Porsche make its way into the lot.

'*Who the fuck is that*,' Blueberry-Loc asked himself as the dude stood up in the driver's seat and jumped out of the Porsche.

Mega Bucks was stunting and he knew it! Not only did he have every bitch in the vicinity checking for him, but this funny looking nigga with dreads was all up in his grill.

"Ayo, careful with that there, It cost me a lot of money," Ramel said, laughing with the bad bitch that approached him.

"Mega Bucks!"

Ramel turned around! The funny looking dude with dreads was still staring at him.

"It's Blueberry-Loc, nigga! You're getting all that money you don't know nobody no more, huh?!?"

"Kev? Get the fuck outta here! The dreads threw me off. I ain't gonna front, I was ready to pull the heat out! I saw you looking at me, I thought you was a faggot or something. Either that, or you was scheming on this hundred thousand dollars worth of jewelry I got on. What's up though?"

"Same shit nigga, different day."

"I know you heard that nigga Jerry Moore home! You still got beef with that nigga?"

Blueberry-Loc got crazy quiet! He would see red just thinking about Jerry Moore! What the fuck was Ramel bringing that nigga name up for?

"I'm not trying to be all in your business or nothing, but I remember what him and that nigga Chandar did to you. That faggot nigga Jerry Moore had the nerve to try to violate *me*... He threw a roll of toilet tissue at me! I was gonna push that nigga shit back to the white meat, but my hustle going too good to hit him! I know where the nigga live at if you want his address, or I got something even better. Chandar be using hangar 19 at Kennedy Airport. He be borrowing a jet from a big wig in Vegas, and when he do, he be keeping it in hangar 19... It's there right now as we speak. I got a homie name Barnard that can make something happen, for a price of course. It's up to you, that's your beef!"

Blueberry-Loc had a crazy look in his eyes! "Set it up for me!"

Nasty Nate left Tara snoring in his hotel room. He jetted to the crib, parked his 350Z, and pulled out the black van. Next, he contacted Jerome, but Jerome said he was busy. He found that strange, but what the fuck! He opted to pick up his man Smalls for the job. Smalls weighed about 300 pounds, no fat, all muscle!

They drove into the cul-de-sac of section 5 in Rochdale, and Nate was happy when he spotted Jerry Moore's red SC430 Lexus parked in the circle. He found an empty parking space three cars behind, and was about to maneuver the van into the space, when he peeped Jerry Moore coming out of building 17.

It was about 3:30 in the morning, so the timing was perfect. Rochdale was deserted!

"Get on point Smalls, there that nigga go right there!"

Nate was on automatic! He jumped out of the van real nonchalant and began walking toward building 17. The element of surprise was on his side, but Jerry Moore was a general! It took a second for it to register, but the black van put the OG on point! Bugsy's killers came in a black van!

Jerry Moore reached for his 40 cal! Nate was looking up at the building walking quickly, too quickly! As they were about to pass each other, the big homie felt a jolt! Then he was falling! He still had his gun in his hand, but he was paralyzed! The black van's sliding door opened, and Smalls gave Nate a hand putting Jerry Moore in the back. They handcuffed him and took his gun, and Nate drove around the circle and back out the cul-de-sac. He was on his way to 97-15 Waltham Street.

Chandar had just hung up the phone with Anthony Orena when Karen walked into the bedroom. Chandar had been in New York for over a month and Mr. Orena needed him back in Nevada.

"Hey, Sunshine!" Chandar addressed Karen in high spirit. It was after 11 AM and Karen just came from her doctor's appointment. She had some news and she didn't know how it would be received.

"Hey, baby."

"What's wrong with you," Chandar asked.

Karen looked like she had something on her mind.

"Nothing,"

"Don't give me that 'nothing' business," Chandar said approaching her. He pulled Karen to him and then continued. "Come ere' and tell Daddy what da matter." Chandar was talking like a child.

"Baby... I'm 8 weeks pregnant." The record scratched! Chandar couldn't believe his ears! Karen was looking at him waiting for him to say something.

"Are you serious?"

"Yes."

Chandar's smile lit up the room and he jumped in the air! "I'm gonna be a father again? Yes!!!" He picked Karen up and swung her around.

"Stop Chandar," Karen laughed.

"Girl, you scared me. You came in here like you were diagnosed with cancer or somethin'."

"I didn't know what you was gonna say."

"I say let's celebrate! We'll celebrate all day and night, because tomorrow I have to get back to Vegas. But when I get back, we celebrate some more! This is the best day of my life!"

"Thank you, Chandar."

"Thank you for what?"

"Thank you for being happy."

The basement was dark! The floor was concrete, water pipes ran overhead, and a boiler sat in the corner. Jerry Moore had a pair of handcuffs on each hand and he was handcuffed to the pipes overhead. The bulletproof vest and oversized white tee he wore were ripped from his body and lay on the damp concrete floor.

Smalls had fun punishing the big homies' body with powerful blows, and the big homie did his best trying to get a kick in. Nate walked up and slapped Jerry Moore so hard that the Big Homie almost forgot his own name! With nothing else to do he coughed up a healthy glob of phlegm and spit in his attackers face!

"Oh, you like to spit on people?" Nate said punching the big homie in the mouth as hard as he could, hurting his own hand in the process. Blood poured from Jerry Moore's mouth!

Nate was about to swing another punch when the light came on in the basement. Blueberry-Loc walked into the room with an iron pipe in one hand and a small nylon bag in the other. He walked up to where Jerry Moore was hanging. He tossed the nylon bag to the side and it landed with a clunk.

"Jerry Moore... Do you know who I am," he asked, looking at Jerry Moore with a hatred that was carefully nourished over a period of years.

The big homie spit a glob of spit mixed with blood into Blueberry-Loc's face. Blueberry-Loc didn't flinch! He didn't even wipe the nasty concoction off. Jerry Moore threw a kick at him, but cuz was unaffected.

The big homie's strength was useless in the position he was in. Blueberry-Loc took the led pipe and slammed it against his stomach.

"AAAARRRRR!"

"That's right, scream! Just like a bitch." Blueberry-Loc dropped the pipe and went over to the nylon bag. He opened it and pulled out a pair of scissors. Jerry Moore watched his every move. Blueberry-Loc smiled and began to snip away at his dreads. He cut until there were no more dreads, and then he pulled out battery operated clippers from the bag and shaved his head. When he was done, he stood before Jerry Moore.

"Do you recognize me now?" Blueberry-Loc asked sounding emotional, " It's Kevin! Kevin Cook! You and Chandar left me for dead! I wasn't fucking with nobody," Kevin was crying as he spoke. "You fucked up my life Jerry… I have migraine headaches that are out of this world. I don't walk, I hobble!"

Kevin Cook stood before Jerry Moore as if he was actually waiting for answers ... answers to questions that he asked himself over and over again for years. Jerry Moore was trying to say something but Kevin couldn't catch what he was saying.

"I can't hear you Jerry Moore, speak up!!!"

"I said, blame Lisa," the big homie was able to mumble.

"What? What??? What the fuck did you say?" Blueberry-Loc was yelling like he was really crazy.

" Blame… Lisa," Jerry Moore said with difficulty.

Blueberry-Loc picked up the pipe and began whacking the big homie's legs like a mad man.

"AAAUUUGGGHHH!!!"

Chandar just finished making love to Karen for the third time when he checked the messages on his phone. He listened to the messages from Jerome and quickly called him back.

"What's good, playa?"

"Listen… you covered my ass in Vegas when you didn't have to. You stopped me from going to war when you didn't have to! We're on 2 different teams, but I fucks with you, Chandar. The C.A.B.B.A.G.E. movement is a good thing and I don't want to mess it up."

"Jerome, talk to me... What's going on," Chandar said, sitting up in the bed. Karen was looking at him.

"He got Jerry Moore!"

"Who got Jerry Moore, I don't understand!"

"Blueberry-Loc! He's William Cook's nephew. Y'all punished him way back in the day. They use to call him Kevin."

The room was spinning around! Chandar dipped his hand in the glass of water on the nightstand by the bed and wet his face.

"Where are they?"

"97-15 Waltham Street. I'll meet you there."

"I'm on the way."

Blueberry-Loc couldn't believe Jerry Moore mentioned Lisa! She had been looking out the window when the incident took place. Sure, she was instigating, but Lisa truly wanted Jerry Moore to stop beating on Kevin.

Blueberry-Loc took a rug cutter out the bag. By now, Jerry Moore was going in and out of consciousness.

"Big homie, I killed Don Chi-Chi," Blueberry-Loc said and sliced him across the chest with the razor.

"I killed Bugsy!" He sliced him again! The skin separated and blood squirted from the wounds. Blueberry-Loc took rubbing alcohol from the bag and doused Jerry Moore's chest with it. The big homie was making noises like a crying dog.

Blueberry-Loc was crazy! He used towels to try and stop the bleeding from Jerry Moore's chest. He didn't want him to bleed to death. Not yet at least!

When the flow of blood seemed slowed down, Blueberry-Loc sent a barrage of punches to Jerry Moore's face. They had beat the big homie to a pulp, it was a wonder he was still alive!

They were interrupted by Nasty Nate's phone ringing. Blueberry-Loc looked at Nate as if he just noticed he was in the room. Nate answered the phone.

"Hello?"

"Nate, open the door."

"Here I come," he said hanging up the phone, and then continued. "That's Jerome, he at the door."

While Nate went to open the door, Blueberry-Loc continued to torture Jerry Moore.

Nate opened the door for Jerome and went downstairs, so he didn't see Chandar standing off to the side.

When Jerome walked into the basement, Blueberry-Loc was poking at Jerry Moore's body, admiring his work.

"It's over, Kev!" Jerome said, and then continued. "You got your get back, now let him go."

Blueberry-Loc looked at Jerome like he was the one that was crazy!

"Hell no, it ain't over! It's over when I say it's over," he yelled.

Chandar stepped into the room. Blueberry-Loc's eyes widened in disbelief.

"Well, well, well... I'm glad you can join the party," Blueberry-Loc said, hobbling to his nylon bag.

Smalls and Nate didn't know what the hell was going on.

Blueberry-Loc pulled out a black .380 and aimed it at Chandar.

"You killed my uncle," he yelled.

Jerome snatched the chrome four-fifth from his waist and aimed it at Blueberry-Loc!

"I said it's over, Kev! You got your revenge!"

Nasty Nate pulled out his nine millimeter and pointed it at Jerome.

"Jerome, what you doing, You switching sides?"

Smalls pulled out his nine millimeter and pointed it at Nate.

"I don't know what the fuck is going on Nate, but Jerome is the big homie of my set... I can't let you do nothing to him!"

Chandar pulled out a snub nose 357 Magnum and pointed it at Blueberry-Loc.

"Come on Kevin! Today seems like a good day to die!"

"Wait a minute," Blueberry-Loc yelled then continued. "Jerome, I paid you good money! I never crossed you! Why the change of heart???"

"Put the gun down and we can talk about it. I just think you're going too far."

"Nate, I'm only gonna tell you one more time. Stop pointing your gun at Jerome," Smalls said.

Nate spun around and aimed his gun at Smalls!

"Why do you keep threatening me?"

"Kev..." Jerome said. "Put the gun down!"

"Tell Chandar first!"

Jerome was losing his patience!

"Chandar, go 'head, lower your gun. If he tries something, he's gonna die too."

Chandar lowered his gun. That's when Jerry Moore coughed, and Nate opened fire on Smalls but Jerome thought it was Blueberry-Loc squeezing off! He emptied the clip in Kevin Cook, knocking him off his feet. Before Nate could turn around, Chandar was blowing holes in his frame!

The smell of gunpowder was in the basement, and a light cloud of smoke lingered in the air.

Chandar found the handcuff keys in Nate's pocket… He opened the cuffs and Jerry Moore fell into his arms. He was still alive!

"We have to leave him," Jerome said.

"I can't," Chandar cried. The tears fell shamelessly.

"Chandar, we have to! We'll call an ambulance, he needs medical attention."

Chandar took deep breaths! Jerome was right. He kissed Jerry Moore on the forehead and laid him down gently.

The sirens could be heard in the distance.

# *Chapter Twenty Six*

A-Blood and Chandar cleared the security checkpoint and walked quickly toward hangar 19. Chandar was deeply distressed and he needed the company, but A-Blood also tagged along because he had something very important he wanted to get off his chest.

The Galaxy Intercontinental Business Jet was fueled and ready to go when they finally got on board. Chandar and A-Blood buckled up in the comfortable recliners and the jet taxied into position on the runway.

Within minutes they were cleared for takeoff, and Chandar felt the familiar powerful thrust of the jet making its way down the airstrip. Once airborne, Chandar swallowed hard a few times in an attempt to unplug his ears.

While A-Blood and Chandar were a mile high in the sky, federal agents was on their way to the hospital. Whether Jerry Moore was stable or not, he was under arrest and being charged with the R.I.C.O. Act. The feds did a series of pre-dawn raids and they had Cue, G-Bundles, Tank, Sarah, and Shan Will in custody, among others. Reggie Ransom was nowhere to be found!

"You know I'm gonna be a father again," Chandar said, attempting to be courteous.

"Karen's pregnant," A-Blood asked, genuinely surprised.

Chandar nodded his head. "Drama! You about to have a little man. I bet you it's a boy!"

"I hope so, fam! I need someone to carry the legacy."

The plane hit an air pocket and experienced a spell of turbulence.

"That's why I don't like to fuck with these small ass planes," A-Blood said looking at the walls and ceiling.

"We gotta die from something," Chandar said prophetically.

The homie was crazy sad! A-Blood was too, but he knew Jerry Moore would pull through. He sat in his recliner searching for the right words to tell Chandar what was on his mind.

The plane hit another pocket, and it shook violently, thats when the pilot's voice came over the intercom.

"Please secure your seatbelts, we're experiencing some difficulties."

A-Blood didn't believe this shit! He knew he should've kept his black ass on the ground with the rest of the sane people. But noooo, he wanted to clear his conscience. He wanted to clear the air with Chandar, but he still didn't get up the nerves to tell him.

"Homie, you know I love you, right," he started.

Chandar looked at him suspiciously.

"Of course... But I don't like conversations that start-"

The plane experienced yet another round of turbulence! This time the lights flickered off and the power shut down! The jet nosedived and quickly began to descend!

"Damn," A-Blood was gripping his seat... the plane was going down! He looked at Chandar with fear in his eyes. "I got something to get off my chest!"

"You better make it fast," Chandar yelled.

"Okay, listen… me and William Cook were friends before I met you."

"And????"

"Well, you know I banged against that nigga when we made the exchange at the train yard! And when Don Chi-Chi tried to get the drop on you, I stopped him, because my loyalty is with U.B.N.; United Bloods in tune."

"A-Blood, we're about to die, fool! Say what you need to say!"

And A-Blood dropped the bomb!

"I was the one who told William Cook where Lucky lived! He tricked me. He told me it wasn't beef! I'm sorry homie… If it wasn't for me, Lisa would probably still be alive."

STEP YA GAME UP PUBLISHING
EVEN FICTION NEEDS TO BE BELIEVABLE!

**P.O. Box 25578 • Charlotte, NC 28229**

# Order Form

Name: _____

Address: _____

City: _____ State: _____ Zip: _____

| Qty. | Title | Price | Total |
|------|-------|-------|-------|
| _____ | Tropical Illusions | $15.00 | _____ |
| _____ | 24 Hours To Live | $15.00 | _____ |
| _____ | Anybody Could Be Touched | $15.00 | _____ |
| _____ | The Star In The Mirror (Coming Soon) | $15.00 | _____ |

Subtotal: _____

Shipping fees: _____

**Total:** _____

Books will be shipped within 7 business days once payment has been processed. All shipments will go out media mail. First book ($3.95); each additional book is $1.50 per book. No personal checks will be accepted. Make institutional checks or money orders payable to: **Step Ya Game Up Publishing** or go to **www.stepyagameuppublishing.com** to place an order.

**Step Ya Game Up Publishing**
EVEN FICTION NEEDS TO BE BELIEVABLE!

## P.O. Box 25578 • Charlotte, NC 28229

# *Order Form*

Name: _____

Address: _____

City: _____ State: _____ Zip: _____

| Qty. | Title | Price | Total |
|------|-------|-------|-------|
| ____ | Tropical Illusions | $15.00 | _____ |
| ____ | 24 Hours To Live | $15.00 | _____ |
| ____ | Anybody Could Be Touched | $15.00 | _____ |
| ____ | The Star In The Mirror<br>(Coming Soon) | $15.00 | _____ |

Subtotal: _____

Shipping fees: _____

**Total:** _____

Books will be shipped within 7 business days once payment has been processed. All shipments will go out media mail. First book ($3.95); each additional book is $1.50 per book. No personal checks will be accepted. Make institutional checks or money orders payable to: **Step Ya Game Up Publishing** or go to **www.stepyagameuppublishing.com** to place an order.

STEP YA GAME UP PUBLISHING
EVEN FICTION NEEDS TO BE BELIEVABLE!

**P.O. Box 25578 • Charlotte, NC 28229**

# Order Form

Name: _____

Address: _____

City: _____ State: _____ Zip: _____

| Qty. | Title | Price | Total |
|------|-------|-------|-------|
| _____ | Tropical Illusions | $15.00 | _____ |
| _____ | 24 Hours To Live | $15.00 | _____ |
| _____ | Anybody Could Be Touched | $15.00 | _____ |
| _____ | The Star In The Mirror (Coming Soon) | $15.00 | _____ |

Subtotal: _____

Shipping fees: _____

**Total:** _____

Books will be shipped within 7 business days once payment has been processed. All shipments will go out media mail. First book ($3.95); each additional book is $1.50 per book. No personal checks will be accepted. Make institutional checks or money orders payable to: **Step Ya Game Up Publishing** or go to **www.stepyagameuppublishing.com** to place an order.

www.ingramcontent.com/pod-product-compliance
Lightning Source LLC
Chambersburg PA
CBHW070008260626
47159CB00005B/1729

\* 9 780985 330316 \*